Dope Dick

FOREVER MINE

Dope Dick

FOREVER MINE

A Novel By

Donald Reynolds

PUBLISHER'S NOTE:

This book is a work of fiction. It is not meant to depict, portray or represent any particular real person. All the characters, incidents, and dialogues are the products of the author's imagination and are not to be construed as real. Any references or similarities to actual events, entities, real people, living or dead, or to real locales are intended to give the novel a sense of reality. Any similarities in other names, characters, entities, places, and incidents, are entirely coincidental. All rights reserved, including the right of reproduction in whole or part in any form.

All Copyrights Reserved © 2021 by Donald Reynolds & Uncaged Minds Publishing

Acknowledgement

First and foremost, I must acknowledge the Almighty. Then there is the beautiful queen who gave birth to me, my mother. My wife my children. The mothers of my children, and my family. And all those I love resting in paradise.

Shout out to my fans and comrades, of which there are too many to name. I must also acknowledge and give sincere gratitude to the book stores who respect and carry urban literature. Thank you for valuing our stories, and our lives. We matter! The magazines: Kite, State VS. Us, GO Viral, Buttz, Publishers Weekly, Hollywood Reporter. San Francisco Bay View. The book clubs, Strong Sisters Book Club, ATL Book Club Babes, and Dave dopest photographer in the world. Now it's time to get to the story!

About The Author

DONALD REYNOLDS graduated from the streets university, summa cum laude. He writes from a raw and unique perspective rarely felt anymore in urban literature. A proud father of eight, he has experienced or seen it all, and has put in more than his share of work in the streets, and in the belly of the beast.

When Reynolds is not writing, he is mentoring, working out, meditating, and polishing up his movie scripts for upcoming film projects. Follow him on Instagram: @uncagedminds

Chapter 1

The murder rate in Chicago was soaring to record numbers again. As Calvin Jones stood there in the day room captivated by the morning news broadcast, he knew he would only be adding to it. "Wait," he growled at a lanky khaki-wearing convict who was trying to change the TV channel. "Don't change that, I'm watching that, G."

"You're about to be out there knee-deep in that west side war zone. We trying to catch the football scores."

At least twelve other men agreed in favor of catching the NFL highlights on ESPN.

Frowning now, Calvin stormed to his lower-tier cell. There was no real need of arguing over the idiot box today. "Fuck them lame ass bitches," whispered Calvin digging his shank out of his Timberland boot. He tossed the perfectly-sharpened steel on his bunk, reminding himself again that this was his last day of incarceration. It didn't seem real. Any other time Calvin would have insisted on a fade. In all of the 3-years he had just served, this particular TV near his cell was the only thing he had control over, and now that control was finally over.

The Greyhound bus ride from Pekin, Illinois' Federal Correctional Institution up to Chicago was to be about 5-hours. Nervous is how Calvin felt. Sick in fact. He glanced down at his G-Shock, realizing that destiny was pulling him closer. Before his mind could drift to what needed to be done there was a sudden knock at his cell door. Calvin came out of the haze of his murderous meditation and standing there was Sanchez. "Come in nigga." They shook up. Sanchez pulled the door shut behind himself.

Sanchez was a smooth Latin King gang member who Calvin normally worked out with. "You ready for the world, it's your time to take the main stage?"

"Ain't no question," replied Calvin. "But you know I need something to numb the soul before I go. Bless my gangsta." Calvin held his palm out, his fingers motioning to give it up.

"You trying to leave this bitch high, huh?" From his pocket, Sanchez pulled up of small piece of wax paper. He carefully unfolded it and gave Calvin a tiny orange triangular-shaped dose of Suboxone. "Here bro." Sanchez folded the wax paper back up. "Do the right thing out there. Stay up."

Calvin's facial expression turned grim, "why lie to you or myself?" He paused just long enough to prepare his dope for consumption. "I got nothing but murder on my mind." After setting the synthetic drug in the valley of a plastic spoon, Calvin added a single drop of water. As the Suboxone dissolved, Calvin admired his muscular reflection in a small mirror above the sink. He was proud of his bedroom body. Over the duration of 36 months, he had bulked up considerably and was playing with 425-pounds on the bench press easily.

Sanchez peered out of the cell window gazing at the expansive prison compound, he could see a crowd of inmates in the distance, heading toward the recreation yard. Sanchez was well-acquainted with Calvin, they had put in some work together two-years ago when a well-known rat arrived on the yard. Without a shadow of doubt, Sanchez knew death would be knocking at someone's door tonight. Calvin had been dealing with so many demons, and now they would be released. "Stay up my nigga. Be safe in the streets," said Sanchez heading toward the cell door.

"Aye," said Calvin. He reached down grabbing his knife off his bunk. "I want you to have my girlfriend." Calvin firmly placed the cruel 10-inch weapon in Sanchez's clutches. "Make it out this bitch alive, get this bitch bloody if you have to. By the time you touch down next year, I'll have a spot at the table for you."

The men embraced. Next, Sanchez tucked the shank on his waistline and left out the cell.

Calvin took the spoon off the desk cautiously not to spill it. Then he snorted the liquid dope up both waiting nostrils. Instantly, his stomach contracted and he gained the numbness he had been yearning for all morning. For what he had planned required the absence of all feelings or emotions.

Chapter 2

Mike Stone kicked his sand-colored ostrich-skinned penny loafers up on his desk. And while fidgeting with his pinky ring, he gazed aimlessly out of the expensive, huge glass windows at the colorful rows of new Lexus automobiles. He was definitely living his best life. Mike laced his fingers together and set his hands on his lap, relishing in his accomplishments. For the past few months, he had outsold every other salesperson by at least a dozen vehicles. Mike had an uncanny way with doing business, but his mother had always told him it was a gift.

On this particular afternoon in Orland Park, Illinois, Mike's thoughts were not exactly on selling any cars. His concerns were more about the woman he had been dating. He loved Deloris, she complimented his confident persona and style. As he thought about her and her 6-year-old daughter, Briana, it caused a bright smile to stretch itself across his dark and handsome face. The thing was, her daughter's daddy was coming home from prison today. "That's a big problem," he confessed to the open space of his plush office.

Mike snatched up the telephone receiver off his oak desk and punched in Deloris' number.

"Hello," she answered.

"What you doing wifey?" asked Mike. His smile grew wider now.

"Just getting Briana ready, she anxious to see her daddy today."

"Is that right?" He paused and frowned. "So you sure it's not going to be no problems with us and our relationship? Guys just coming home from the joint want familiar vagina."

"Boo, like I explained a hundred times before, me and Cal ain't together. He walked out on me when he went away to prison. We're going to co-parent. That's it. I am completely and totally in love with you Michael, didn't I prove this last night?" Deloris giggled, praying to diffuse Mike's concerns.

Mike sighed. "Deloris, I'm not trying to sound too insecure, I just want to be sure we're on the same brain frequency. I've got my life invested in what we're building together."

"I understand sweetheart," she cooed. "I love you. You complete me and I would never cheat on you. Do you love me? Do you trust me?"

Mike said "with all of my heart. I gotta run. I'll call you later."

After disconnecting the call, Mike glanced at his Rolex, then dialed up a trusted associate who repossessed cars for him all throughout the state. He owed Mike a favor and there was no better time to collect than now. The repo man answered with a familiar baritone voice.

Mike cleared his throat. "Listen, I need you at the Greyhound, downtown. Keep your eyes on that fool. Shit's not feeling right with my instincts."

"Yeah. I know, we talked about this, I'm on the way there now Mike."

The line went dead.

Mike had done his homework on Calvin Jones thoroughly. He knew the streets of Chicago called him Killa Cal. Calvin Jones had beat two bodies in the state, before the feds settled for indicting him for the pistol. Instead of risking a 10-year statutory maximum sentence, Calvin coped out to 36-months. Mike also felt he was on his way home with ill-intentions of rebuilding his life with Deloris. But Deloris, she belonged to him now and if Calvin ever got her back, it would be over Mike's dead body. She was the goddess of his dreams. To clear his thoughts, Mike walked out onto the bustling car lot in search of a customer.

While assisting a young couple with the financing of a pre-owned vehicle, Mike's cellphone buzzed at his hip, "yeah?" he answered.

"Somebody just picked that big young nigga up at the bus station in a Cadillac Escalade — a black one, dealer tag, tinted glass. A bootylicious chick with a long blonde weave job."

"Follow him," said Mike. "Yeah, follow him... for the rest of the night." After Mike inserted his cellphone into his shirt pocket, he keyed in a credit application. He was nervous, but at the same time, there was money to be made on the job. He trusted Deloris and knew they would be making love tonight. Mike grinned. He knew it wouldn't be shit to give the green-light to get Calvin knocked off. Killing in Chicago was like taking candy from a baby. But it was something he had never done. Mike's grin transformed into a deal-sealing smile when he noticed the couple before him had a credit score of 780. He handed them a contract and a set of keys. "Sign here."

***

Deloris had always had a fetish for drug dealers. In the late 80s, her father sold cocaine but his empire crumbled apart when she turned sweet 16; when Chicago Police murdered him. So dating Mike was so much different. He was all legal and all hers, and checking a serious bag. What she loved most of all is he spoiled her and her daughter with attention and gifts.

On the surface, Mike offered her the same money-ain't-a-thang lifestyle, minus the fears and anxieties that came with dope dealers. Deloris never had to worry about Mike being murdered in the streets or getting locked up. Twelve years had gone by and the painful loss of her father was an emotional scar that never healed.

While driving her new snow-white Lexus SUV, Delores gazed over at her daughter, Briana. She sat in the passenger seat. Deloris could tell by the child's facial expression that she couldn't wait to be in her daddy's arms. Yet at the same time, Deloris had a dark secret. She was not totally sure if Briana was in fact Calvin's biological child. She had gone through her fair share of men in the past. She closed the door to those soul-haunting thoughts. "You ready to see your Daddy?"

"Yes! Ma yes! I miss him so much." Briana bounced up and down on the peanut-butter-colored leather seats.

Deloris smiled, she knew the feeling of being a 'Daddy's Girl.' After making a right-hand turn onto 117th, off of Halsted, Deloris parked in front of a brick recently-renovated, three-story apartment building, she thumbed in a number on her cellphone letting Calvin's mother know they had arrived. Deloris was planning on leaving Briana there to spend some much-needed quality time with her father. "Don't you give your grandma no problems either, you understand me?"

Briana motioned with her head that she understood, her cute colorful hair beads click-clacked together. Briana inhaled a gust of optimism, anticipating the arrival of her father.

After leaving, Deloris weaved her way through heavy traffic, eventually arriving back home. While in the driveway, she killed the silent engine. The sudden arousing thought of Calvin being free came to mind, causing her to fan her thighs. Deloris closed her cat-like eyes, considering the forbidden idea of hooking up with Calvin. She bit her glossy bottom lip. Before she knew it, her hand was already down inside her panties, slow-strumming her clit. She could never deny the fact that Calvin was the best lover she had ever encountered. With her legs now trembling, she pulled her hand out of her split, it was drenched, as was her panties. Deloris headed into her home to finish what she started.

***

Behind the steering wheel of the sleek black Caddy truck was Calvin's ex-girlfriend named Camille; she eased the SUV along the curb in front of an older-styled brown house on the Westside.

"Right here," whispered Calvin. His eyes studied a dispersing group of junkies, then the house.

From out of the darkness emerged two hooded men, both cautious to approach the Escalade. With wide open arms, Calvin climbed down out of the passenger side man-hugging the duo. "Whudd up doe?" Calvin smiled.

One of the men fired up a Newport. He flicked his dreads to the back and said, "shit." He exhaled a plume of grey smoke. "Good to see you."

The other said, "Nigga, you got big as fuck!"

All three chuckled for a second. But all of the laughs came to an end when Camille circled up. She had hips and ass, and a juicy set of pink traffic-stopping lips. She kept a straight face, then blew a bubble with the chewing gum in her mouth.

"Yall come on in," said the taller of the two men.

Everyone walked inside.

The place was nothing but a dope trap. Cigar guts laid strewn all over the coffee table and on the hardwood floors. On an end table, rested two large stainless-steel pistols and a digital scale. Two young light-skinned dudes thumbed away on joysticks, playing Call of Duty, one had a blunt in his mouth dangling from his lips. Both men paused the game to salute Calvin and the sexy lady who accompanied him. "About damn time they let you out," said one of the men.

"Yeah well I lost all my good time. I ended up maxing out."

Before long, all four men willingly broke bread. Calvin handed the rubber-banded knots of cash to Camille. She pushed it all down in her Chanel purse, careful not to disturb the trigger on the pistol that was in there. Calvin knew what he'd been given was only a small fraction of what they all had stolen from him during his incarceration. When the blunt came his way, Calvin hit it hard. It was time to do what he'd come here to do. His stomach growled, urging him on.

Camille was just standing there looking delicious and smelling like Dolce & Gabana. All she awaited was the signal. She continued chewing her bubble gum and blowing bubbles until finally Calvin passed her the blunt. Then he winked at her.

Guilt was so thick in the air that Calvin couldn't wait another minute but he played it cool and calm and cold.

"Is there a bathroom in here?" asked Camille.

"In the back on the right," said one of the men thumbing on a joystick. As Camille sashayed past the TV, he couldn't help but take pleasure in her shapely ass. His cellphone began to vibrate and as he read the text his eyes grew wide. He looked at the LCD display again, he set the joystick down then examined the text.

"You rat ass bitch, you're a dead man tonight," was displayed from an unknown phone number.

Calvin could tell by the way the man responded to the text message Camille had just sent him that he knew what time it was. Calvin noticed his red suspicious eyes cut across the living room. They made eye contact and it became a thirty-second mind-reading exercise; one that explained it all.

"What y'all niggas selling out here, dog?" asked Calvin, his stomach barking and growling.

"Fuck yeah. Blow, coke, crack, meth, roxies, oxy. We eating out this bitch."

By this time, Camille came into view aiming her compact Glock. "Don't nobody move an inch!" she spat.

One of the men thought it was a game, he reached for the pistol sitting on the table, but two unforgiving slugs tore his face open, sending him twisting to the floor. Calvin crossed one leg over the other, his ears ringing, as the pool of crimson-red blood formed wider and wider. Camille trained her pistol on the man with the joystick.

It had been a while since Calvin had heard the clapping of gunfire, unlike Camille. She looked mouth-watering standing there, thought Calvin. Smiling, full of confidence, Calvin took hold of the two pistols off the table. They were Taurus-made identical, both .40 calibers. He thumbed the firearms into the firing position, disengaging the safety buttons.

"First," said Calvin looking directly at one of the men. "I'm about to send you to hell tonight. You rat bitch. Yeah, I saw your statements and name all in my paperwork." Calvin probed the depths of the man's eyes, he could sense the calmness of his soul.

"Bitch, I'm not about to deny what the fuck I did. I been accepted what I got coming. I'm not about to beg you for my life bitch nigga. Pussy nigga, death don't scare me. I fucked your bitch ass baby mama too and was planning on fucking your daughter. I'd—"

Calvin slapped the side of the man's face with the Taurus sending teeth flying across the room. The man spit out a tooth, then spit a glob of blood on Calvin's chest.

"Yeah, I told pussy nigga. I'd do it again too if—"

Boc! Boc! Boc!

Camille couldn't take in another word the opp was saying. The three rounds she sent through his head left the man frozen stiff with a startled expression plastered on his face. A thick blanket of gunpowder clung in the air along with the tormenting dread of more death. The goddess with the Glock found the next victim's chest as a perfect bull's eye.

Boc! Boc!

With his mouth agape, the dying man gasped for oxygen, but his own blood quickly filled his lungs up like water balloons, leaving him trembling and drowning until he expired.

"Where the dope and the snaps at my nigga?" barked Calvin. "You already know I need all of that."

"In the back bedroom," the last man alive replied. "I'll take you to it."

It was all too easy, Calvin was taken to a perfectly-designed floor safe that set underneath a condom-filled nightstand. After the safe was opened, Calvin afforded the cooperating man, on his knees the opportunity of whispering a farewell prayer. It was what it was, but Calvin had questions. He needed answers. "Yall just left me for dead, huh, Joe?" Calvin crashed one of the pistols across the man's face.

"Please Cal," he pleaded looking up fearfully into the barrel of the pistol leveled on his face. "I gave your bitch the money I owed you bruh. All the times I hit shorty off! This ain't for us. Let me live! We grew up together my nigga. Our mothers go to church together."

Calvin's pulse raced and yet he knew tonight he'd reached the point of no return. "You was fucking my bitch Deloris wasn't you? Keep it one-hunnid?"

"That alley-rat bitch ain't shit! You got locked up, she sold all your shit. All your cars, jewels, clothes, guns. On God, I ain't fuck her, Cal. She fucking on this model-type square nigga who manage… the Lexus dealership in Orland Park! Fuck that hoe man. This over a hoe?"

Calvin used the barrel of the pistol to push his long-time friend's face away. He couldn't look him in the eyes. Never before had he witnessed him cry like this. Not even when his brother got killed when they were 8 years old. "Yeah, my hoe."

"Look me in my eyes before you kill me nigga," he yelled. "We brothers!"

Boc! Boc! Boc! The ghetto brother's blood and brain properties trailed down a nearby wall, while a slow-rolling tear trickled its way down Calvin's face. He gathered all of the spoils of the robbery, wrapping it all in a semen-stained bed sheet.

Calvin found Camille in the living room rifling through the pants pockets of the deceased men sprawled on the floor. The soles of her white Nikes were blood-red in spite of her best efforts to avoid the lakes of blood that covered the floor. One of the dead men had a diamond encrusted chocker around his neck, that quickly became Camille's, as did his pistol that she found at his waistline. "Bae let's go," she said, donning the chain around her neck.

Like nothing ever happened, they casually ventured out into the night, got into the SUV and made a perfect get away.

Not too far behind the Escalade the repo man followed, all the while reporting what he saw and suspected to Mike on his cellphone. He knew the sound of gunfire and could have sworn he heard "at least ten to twelve explosions."

Calvin exhaled, he felt alive again, born again. He felt like the servant of death. More than anything else right now, he wanted to release the pressure of three years of sexual deprivation. And calm the rumbling in his stomach. He knew the dog food would handle that.

En route to a distant motel, Calvin prepared his misogynistic mind for the future and his fate. He knew

Camille had a man, and a starving gorilla riding her back that demanded to be fed. Calvin didn't give a fuck about none of that. He reached over, tugging Camille's thighs open a bit. During the entire drive to the motel, he used his fingers to prime her centerpiece, and just simply enjoyed the thrill of his new found freedom.

Chapter 3

On Cicero Avenue near the airport is where Camille rented a cheap hotel room. There, she kicked off her bloody Nikes and took off her socks. She let her hair down and continued to undress.

Meanwhile, Calvin was dumping out bundles of cash on the bed. Coke, weed, baggies filled with pills poured out too, followed by what he'd hoped to find. It was heroin, dog food. In unison, he and Camille smiled at each other. It looked to be about six ounces. It was a tan-white color, compressed into chunks.

"I need a hit killer Cal," cooed Camille, completely naked by now. She'd noticed blood speckles on her clothes, and it was caked against the diamond chain round her neck to too. Two, full perky breasts were cupped by her own hands now. "We did damn good," she added, her brown eyes appraising the night's take.

"I need a hit too baby girl." Calvin laughed. "I'm fresh out of prison with four bodies already under my belt." He used his fingernail to scoop up a bump. Then he snorted it. Then he did it again up the other nostril. He turned toward his lady of the night and handed her the bag of dope. As Camille carefully took the bag, Calvin felt the strong effects of the dog food. His limp body forced him to the bed where he slumped over into the throes of a nod. The mighty dope felt as if it transported him to what felt like heaven.

Camille sat down beside Calvin and she too hit the dust, twisting her nose. The cash and piles of narcotics caught her eyes. Then she frowned at Calvin's pathetic nod. "You got me all wet... Calvin?" She stood, removed his Timbs. Then his blood-splattered pants, after removing the pistols from his pockets. Next, slowly she pulled his boxers off.

For three years she had waited for the thick, long penis she now held in her slow-stroking hand. Upon maneuvering to her knees she continued the hand-job, she then filled her mouth with both his hairy balls. Her hand felt his dick growing as he responded to her love. Still jacking him seductively, her tongue slithered between the crack of his ass. "I missed this big ass dick Calvin," she whispered to his penis that was firm and fully erect. Without further delay, she inserted his manhood into her mouth, which she slowly popped it out. Then spit on it and reinserted it. Faster, now she rode him with her face, hitting the back of her throat. Camille took a second to relax her gag reflexes, allowing for deeper facial penetration. She cradled his balls trying in vain to deep throat Calvin's massive dick. Her saliva ran down his pole causing it to glisten. Again, her tongue sought out his virgin asshole, till finally her tongue penetrated him.

Calvin started drifting back to Chicago and the reality of his life. The dope was torch and Camille was trying her best to enhance his pleasure. She started sucking his stiff member again, fast and deep, and a tear fell from her chin. With no hands she sucked on, damn near about to vomit. His dick expanded the depths of her throat. She could see Calvin looking at her face, his pleading eyes begging for contact with hers. Next Camille tried her best to stuff it all in her neck again. She moaned as if what she was doing gave her the greatest joy. Camille felt Calvin's strong black hands gripping her head, his hips pumped in beautiful sync with her lovemaking head-bobble. This is what she enjoyed, pleasing. She was finally feeling a oneness with Calvin. He forced her further down until she totally gave in, he ignored the snot that drained from her nose. He put it all in her, every inch.

***

The night hadn't gone the way Mike had planned it at all. Deloris was upset and had an attitude. Calvin had the nerve to stand Briana up after she was so excited to see him today. "I'm sorry," she told Mike. "I'm not in the mood for sex."

Mike wasn't tripping, he tried to comfort his queen by spooning her. He knew she loved being held this way. The thing was, spooning Deloris always caused him to form an aching erection. His penis could feel the heat of her vagina as it sat helplessly at the gates of it. He kissed the back of her neck. "Briana's a big girl. Maybe something came up, Deloris," he whispered.

Deloris didn't respond.

"Maybe we should take an out-of-town trip this weekend. The three of us," suggested Mike.

Still no reply. Deloris was like that. When she would get upset, she'd become totally introverted.

"I wish I could get inside your head sweetheart," whispered Mike, feeling his erection slowly deflating. Mike gave some deep thought to what all he had been told earlier about Calvin's movements. Gunshots and fleeing the scene with a chick in an Escalade. In a way, it was a relief to know Calvin was with some other chick getting his rocks off. Too bad Briana was disappointed. Poor child didn't deserve it.

By now, Deloris was giving off a slight snore. Mike came to terms that he wouldn't be getting any loving tonight and it was all because of some shit her ex failed to do. "I knew he was going to be a problem," whispered Mike. His mind turned toward some plans to solve his problem before it got out of control. The vibrating of his cellphone startled him. Mike snatched it off the nightstand. His repo man's incoming number flashed. In a barely-audible tone he answered "yeah."

"You not gonna believe this shit but I doubled-back to that house on the west side, the cops got the motherfucker yellow-taped off and brought out four fucking dead bodies. Your girlfriend's dude's a cold killer Mike. You better watch your back, pussy ain't worth dying over, not with so many single bitches out here, praying for good men... hardworking men like us."

"Damn," said Mike. "Dead bodies?"

"Damn, is right. You'll be a damn fool to continue fucking with—"

Mike ended the call and sat up on the edge of the bed. He gripped his head between both hands. Then he tapped the Chicago news app to get more details and information. To his dismay, shit was real and he was afraid.

***

Camille loved how hot, thick and lengthy Calvin's bedroom muscle was, she yanked it out her mouth, catching her breath. It was beautiful. Veins rippled all throughout it. Her wet vagina pulsated in anticipation of riding it tonight. She pulled up the baggie with the dope in it, pinched a small amount of it and sprinkled his chocolate bar. Then using her tongue, she sent some of it down into the valley of his pee hole. After she rubbed it against her face, it went back into her mouth. With both hands, Camille worked his manhood, up, down, up, down. It couldn't get any harder. "I'm ready to feel this dope dick, baby."

Holding Calvin's dick made her hands seem tiny. Calvin's head literally dangled from the center of his shoulders, yet his hips moved back and forth involuntarily.

He could see Camille mounting him, but it was all like a fantasy. Her caramel-skinned face contorted as if it were killing her. The feeling of being stretched by his girth was amazing. She loved painful sex and wanted it to hurt. With all her body weight slamming down the way it was, she began to release a series of squirts. Plop!

All Calvin could do was observe the way it was all unfolding tonight. His eyelids closed shut. The clapping music their bodies made combined with Camille's screams didn't seem real.

"I love it. I love this dope dick!" Camille was nimble, she used both hands, pulling her ass cheeks apart. She wanted every bit, nothing less. Tonight she killed men for the rights to it. She shuddered, feeling the surging of a tsunami working its way down. "Cal! baby. Baby! I'll kill a bitch over this dick. This my dick! This my-ah-ah-ah!" sang Camille. Her body violently shook from right to left as she slowed the pace, she sank her claws into the mound of chest muscle Calvin offered. Her body dripped perspiration, sparkled and glistened.

Camille glanced down at the bed-soaked mess her ejaculation created. She gingerly allowed him out of her satisfied hole, where his long dripping dick plopped on his six pack. "Shit, boy. See what that dick do to me?"

Calvin didn't answer. He couldn't. Drool hung down from the corner of his mouth, while he teetered on the verge of an overdose. Camille held her lower tummy, then used the bed comforter to wipe away the wetness on her thighs, ass and all in between her vagina. "I've got a curfew. I need to get home to my nigga."

Camille dressed herself as fast as she could. Calvin was still somewhat incapacitated by the dog food and good pussy. Camille helped herself to what she knew she deserved for all she had done tonight. Besides, she did most of the killing anyway.

After taking one of the twin pistols and what she wanted, Camille kissed Calvin on his forehead. "Welcome home, baby boy."

After firing up the Cadillac SUV, Camille unraveled the bag of dope, took another bump and headed toward the south suburbs. She couldn't wait to give the diamond chain to her man. That was the least she could do for the man who put up with her bullshit and her addiction.

Calvin wiped the slobber from his mouth. His eyes drowsily scanned the empty room. It somewhat reminded him of the cell he had left behind that morning, only a bit nicer, and a little scarier. Being alone in the room with drugs and a gun caused paranoia to settle in. He grabbed the motel room's phone and dialed Deloris' number. She didn't pick up. He tried again. A proper-talking male answered. "Who the fuck is this?" asked Calvin. "Put Delo on the phone."

There was no reply. Her line went dead.

"Hello! Hello," yelled Calvin, pissed. He hammered the phone down, then hit the dog food again.

Chapter 4

By the time Deloris woke up, Mike was already gone to work. She could still smell his Dior cologne lingering in the air. After crawling out of bed Deloris pulled her bedroom curtains wide open and thanked God for another day.

The fact that Calvin could be so insensitive had drained her emotionally last night. She felt guilty for not satisfying Mike's sexual needs, but with Deloris, sex was more mental than physical and her mind just wasn't there at all. She grabbed her cellphone off the nightstand and dialed up Briana. The child didn't answer. It was still early. Instead, she thumbed in Calvin's mother's number. She picked up and by the happiness of her voice it was evident she was in a cheerful mood. Deloris figured Calvin must have finally shown up.

"Hey Momma," said Deloris. She had always called Calvin's mother 'Momma', because at one point in time, she saw 'forever' in her son's eyes and besides, her own mother had moved down to Indianapolis to marry a man she had met at a church retreat six-years ago. "How are you this morning?"

"Blessed chil'."

"Did Calvin show up?" Deloris knew the answer but asked anyway.

"Yes, four-something in the morning, he's here asleep and Briana's right there by his side. That girl loves her father."

"I know you're happy to see him. I hear it in your voice." Deloris smiled.

"He better sit his butt down somewhere, get a job and join the church. Hold on, here he is."

There was a pause. Deloris sat on the edge of her bed. She cleared her throat.

"Hello, what's good Delo?" asked Calvin.

Deloris couldn't help but to smile. "I'm good. How are you Calvin? And welcome home."

"I'm glad as a muthafucka to be out that living hell. But it would be better though, if I was there with you instead of on my mother's couch. Before going to prison I had a house."

"Oh Lord, I wrote you long before you even got out Calvin and told you I was now in a serious relationship and might be getting married."

"Yeah," said Calvin. "You did that, I got your 'Dear John Letter', respect. Look, when I left, I had clothes, four whips, a safe full of coke and jewelry, where my shit at?"

Deloris knew this topic would come up. Her Comeback was scripted and memorized. "You know when you left, I had to move out the house, them niggas you was beefing with knew where me and your daughter lived. I had no choice but to sell nearly everything and pay your lawyer, get us a new place." What she told him was actually true and the truth, as painful as it was, Deloris had a high standard of living. Gucci, Prada, Fendi, Chanel, Armani, Jimmy Choo, Cartier, Louis Vuitton, Calvin gave her the world; a world she couldn't walk out of in the spur of the moment.

"Yeah, I hate that. I need to see you, come though. I'm trying to buy a used car. I need a ride over to Tony's Auto Mall in Harvey."

"Why can't Momma take you? I've got to run some errands for my pastor." Deloris smiled. She knew for him to be asking to see her that there was still some love there. Then too; she had to catch herself because she was touching herself again. She panted, her thumb stimulated the side of her clit slowly. For some reason she felt aroused that after 3 years of neglecting him, he still needed her. Empowering, she thought.

"Momma and Bri supposed to be going shopping. Please, Delo. You ain't been there for a real nigga since I been gone. All I'm asking for is a ride. Drop me off at the dealership and I'm cool from there."

Deloris couldn't deny him. How could she? Calvin had been through hell and back. And all he wanted was a ride, as she thought about it, this would be her perfect opportunity too, to show him how good she was living without him. He would always tell her she would be nothing without him. Plus, Deloris couldn't wait to show off her new Brazilian butt lift and $2,000-dollar custom Malaysian weave she just had done the other day. "I guess I can do that. I'll be there."

She allowed the multi-jet showerhead to pelt her body into a state of pure calm and bliss. Her mind fought off all the loving memories she once shared with Calvin, but on this morning, fighting her desires was the last thing she wanted to do. She couldn't help but to give in, with her middle finger, Deloris found her G-Spot. She pressed it. Then again, and again and soon came a release that dribbled down her caramel-colored thighs. At that point, she decided against showing up. Naturally, one thing would lead to another and for the most part, she had been a faithful woman to Mike. Her knight in shining armor was Mike and Calvin was her past.

After drying off, Deloris phoned Calvin's Momma to cancel the ride she'd agreed to give. *Instead, I'll go take my man lunch.* She put on some Fendi, a skirt and matching sneakers, all black in color and with her purse, Deloris headed for the front door. She never expected Calvin to be right there and forcing himself inside. She jumped clear out of her skin at the sight of him. "What the fuck are you—" Her eyes zeroed in on the large pistol in his right hand. "Oh my God, no!"

"Where's your little boyfriend at?" He offered Deloris a fake smile. "What's wrong you stinking bitch? Surprised to see me?"

"You got to leave! I didn't invite you over here. Get out Calvin! Now!" She pointed dead at the front door. "Out!"

Calvin back-handed Deloris causing her to stumble backwards, but he snatched her by the weave and pulled her close to him. "Who in the fuck you think you talking to like that huh?"

She didn't have a reply. The taste of blood in her mouth kept her silent and submissive. Calvin, with his full lips twisted, yanked her toward a plush burgundy leather sofa. He spun her and shoved her forward, forcefully bending her over. By now, her butt enhancements inspired an erection and his large flesh-gripping hands explored her soft plump booty. He slapped her ass hard.

"Don't! Please... Stop!"

"Shut the fuck up stupid bitch! This my goddamn pussy bitch. Fuck you thought?"

Calvin snatched her black stringy thong over to the side revealing the hairless vagina that he loved so much and hated at the same time. Using his left hand, Calvin eased his pistol into his pocket. Her shapely bottom mesmerized him and the thought of another man enjoying his treasure chest only caused more fury. He ripped the thong off all together, "I fucking made you!"

"I'm calling the po—"

Smack! Calvin slapped her ass again. "Don't act like you don't want this dick." He placed the tip of his thumb at the rim of her asshole. It was gorgeous and shaped like a tiny star. Her pussy was wet. Calvin pulled up a small jab of dog food, worked out his hefty and starved erection and sprinkled the dope all over the length of his dick. "Delo," he whispered to her. "You are forever mine, bitch." Calvin pushed into Deloris' vagina as violently as he could. She was sopping wet in fact and he knew she would be. She always was.

"I hate you! I hate you!" cried Deloris trying her best to escape his thrusts that came hammer-hard and fast. Easily he overpowered her, forcing her to feel his pain and presence.

"Take this big dick and hate it then," grunted Calvin laying down nearly a foot of fresh-out-of-prison beef in her. His rock-hard six-packed abs smacked repeatedly against her bubble-shaped booty. Gripping her hair like the reins on a stallion, Calvin continued pumping in and out of Deloris with the might of many men. He could feel her struggling body going weak now and blood covered his penis. He couldn't believe Deloris had acted the way she had during those long three punk-ass years. He continued nailing her limp body to the leather sofa, pushing his thumb completely into her ass. "I missed this stinking ass... pussy." Harder, he stroked her.

Deloris was the only woman he had ever given his heart to and she fucking broke it. Calvin began to feel the depressant effects of the dope, as well as the way Deloris' vagina was delivering a series of spasms. He knew she was climaxing, he pushed his thumb in her ass for as it could go, as well as his long blood-laden dick. This was Calvin's way of restoring his heart. He eased his manhood completely out and guided it like a missile straight into her barely-lubricated ass.

Deloris wasn't moving, except for when Calvin's body made impact with hers. He clenched his teeth and made the ugliest fuck-face in the world. Trembling in the fog of heroin and revenge, he reached his long-awaited orgasm. His penis throbbed in sync with her vagina. "Forever mine, Delo forever mine." He kissed the back of her neck. "I hate you too," he confessed.

Calvin pulled his pleasure stick out and used Deloris' cute skirt to wipe the red glaze off. He spanked her booty playfully, leaving her unconscious and slumped ass up over the sofa. Before leaving out, he noticed a fraudulent family photo sitting on the mantel of a bricked fireplace. In the photo was Deloris, Mike and Briana. He shook his head in disappointment taking the photo with him out to the black Escalade where Camille awaited him with a pistol on her lap. "Let's bounce boo." Camille put the SUV in reverse and eventually pulled away down the street.

"Damn, you smell like ass and pussy." Camille let down both windows as they laughed at what just took place. "You stink!"

***

Mike pushed a new pair of solid gold-framed Cartier shades on his nose, he was taking an hour lunch break and wanted to talk face-to-face with his repo man. They met up at the mall not far from the car dealership.

"Sticks what's up?" asked Mike sitting across from him in the food court. He got the name 'Sticks' from his younger days of being involved in gunplay, but today Mike could tell something was on his mind.

"Man, I don't know," he told him. Sticks evaded eye contact. "I guess...last night kind of fucked me up. I haven't slept a wink all night." Sticks finally looked Mike in the face. "We been dogs since high school, this nut you had me follow killed four men, not one, not two. Four! I'm an unwilling witness. It all just threw me like a motherfucker." Sticks sighed.

"I don't blame you," said Mike. "I'm going to handle him myself." He took a bite of his corned beef sandwich.

"Why not get you a bunny my brother and leave them ghetto bitches in the gutter of poverty where they belong?" Sticks took a gulp of his Pepsi. "Life's great on the white side, no conflict. No drama. No friction. No senseless killings. I fuck when I want. Do what I want and it's a beautiful situation." Sticks motioned his head in the direction of white female shoppers coming out of Gap. "Look around you bro you don't see no stupid ass niggers waving guns and shooting."

Mike laughed at Sticks. He knew his comment came from the heart. "You're always going to be my nigga." He laughed again. "But I like my women black, you feel me. The darker the better."

"That sounds good but check it out," said Sticks. He leaned in closer. "Why not just report his ass to the cops, let them do away with him. Fuck! A quadruple homicide and on the day he comes home from prison. Drop a dime, he'll never see daylight. You and your black queen can live happily ever after."

"See. That's what I'm not going to do. That's snitching homie. Where we come from, snitches come up missing. White America's fucking with your head. No matter how much white pussy you get, you'll always be a nigga. Don't switch codes on me my nigga."

Sticks knew he was bogus for even making such a "snitching' remark. "You got a valid point, homeboy. I was dead wrong." Sticks dropped his head and sought out something to say that would change the topic of their conversation. "You got any repos? I'm done trailing murderers. My days of ignorant thuggin' been over. All I wanna do is make beautiful mixed babies, get fat and root for the Cubs." Sticks cradled his protruding stomach.

Mike shook his head, when just then, his cellphone chimed on his hip. He knew it was Deloris and so did Sticks. He placed the phone up to his ear. His eyes grew wide and red. He stood up. "Calm down baby," he said caringly. "I'm on my way!" Mike frowned. "That bitch ass nigga just showed up at my crib and raped Deloris. Fuck! He's a dead man." Mike's stare aimed at Sticks. "I'ma call you later."

Sticks sat there and watched Mike as he slow-trotted through the mall toward the exit. He felt sorry for Mike and wasn't buying the 'rape.' Not at all. He unsnapped his phone from his belt and called to check on his wife. As usual, Amy was home nurturing the kids, barefooted and pregnant, and waiting on him to bring his ass home. He didn't want or need the problems Mike dealt with. "Fuck that shit," he whispered to himself. He caught a full-figured blonde across the food court winking at him. Sticks waved her over, knowing already that she wanted some chocolate. Mike wasn't thinking with his big head, thought Sticks. *Not at all.* The friendly blonde sat beside him and they got acquainted.

Chapter 5

Deloris crawled as best as she could on her knees toward the bathroom. Along the way she collapsed a couple of times. Never in her life had she felt this way. Calvin had literally fucked her into another dimension of existence. For a while she just rested right there on the cold tiled bathroom floor, clutching her vagina, as the bathtub filled up with hot water and began overflowing.

After getting into the tub, Deloris simply enjoyed the total-body sensation of what she just endured. Although it was violent and also considered rape in the eyes of the law, it was the best sex of her life, she thought. She was sore, yet her insides continued to pulsate. Deloris dimmed her heavy eyelids and prayed Calvin didn't knock her up. She felt he did, he was too deep in her guts to misfire like Mike had been doing. The line between love and hate was even thinner now. Her nerves slowly began to settle around the same time she shamefully felt her body yearn for round two. Someone was coming her way. She could hear footsteps.

"Deloris! Baby are you okay?" Mike fell down to his knees. "I got here as fast as I could sweetie. Tell me what happened?" Tears filled the wells of his eyes. His mind questioned the red-tinted tub of water, but the speckles of blood on the floor told the story too well.

"My bitch ass baby daddy," she started crying. "He slapped me, yanked me by my hair, bent me over the couch and raped me!" Mike's stomach turned, he felt totally encapsulated by fury. "You want to go to the hospital, bae?" He kissed her forehead. "How did he know where we live?"

"I don't know. I'll be just fine. That dumb ass bast—"

"Tell me what happened?" He used his forearm to wipe a tear away that ran down his chin. The look on Deloris' face exuded a strange display of satisfaction.

"I did already! He fucked me in my ass too. I hate that...that."

"What?"

"Help me out the tub, honey."

Mike lifted Deloris up and gave her his strong arm to hold and slowly, he led her down the hallway into the bedroom. On the edge of the bed, she rested her wet tender bottom. Mike exited the bedroom and returned with a large, soft body towel. He carefully toweled her dry. The bruise across her face only angered him even more. "I'm Killing that hoe ass nigga," whispered Mike. "You hear me?"

"Mike I'm sorry," she cooed wiping her tears away. "Briana must have told him where we live." She held the lower part of her stomach, then rolled into a fetal ball. "My stomach hurt."

"Look baby..." Mike noticed the red handprint on her ass and damn near choked. "Look, now do you need to go to the hospital?" He folded his arms across his chest, furiously.

She didn't reply. She laid there and started dozing off. Full of disgust and guilt, Mike covered her naked and violated body with a comforter. He knew what he was getting himself into from the jump and yet his manhood would be at stake if he didn't retaliate. His thoughts took a sharp turn to the day they first met on a dating app. Deloris was honest. She told him about the "Monster" who didn't value human life. The "street nigga" who turned women out with his big dick. Mike found her cellphone, scrolled through it. He pulled an ink pen out his pocket and then scribbled down incoming and outgoing phone numbers. After that he swiped into her Facebook page, searching for clues, digging for answers. *Was this consensual sex or rape?* Mike tossed the phone down and stormed back into the bedroom, Deloris was snoring now and didn't want to be bothered. Calvin's heroin-laced dick put her at peace. He picked up her phone again and pocketed it.

"You ain't acting like somebody who has been raped." Mike shook her shoulder. "Deloris?" She pulled away covering her shoulder with the comforter. "Baby, I'm tired, my pussy hurts, hold me."

Mike said "I'm not in the fucking mood to hold you Deloris. I'll be back!" He changed into a fitted all-black Dior jogging suit. But before leaving home, he dug his never-fired Heckler & Koch .45 out of his suit closet. The clip was loaded with Teflon tips. He chambered a round, tucked the pistol in the small of his back and jumped in Deloris' truck. Then he headed to do what needed to be done on this strange night in Chicago.

The way Deloris was acting wasn't exactly adding up. Her energy didn't feel the same. The way she curled up in bed with the contentness of a baby with a fresh pamper didn't sit well. That nigga trashed that pussy, his mind whispered. His palms became sweaty because in his heart he felt it was Deloris' fault or maybe it was his. "Why am I even tripping over some pussy anyway, I got wealthy women throwing ass at me all day every day at work," he said to no one at all. Mike parked up the block from Calvin's mother's apartment building. He knew he would catch the rapist slippin' there, or at least he hoped to.

A little more than thirty-minutes had gone by, Mike fired up the truck and eased away from the curb. A group of young gang bangers had grown suspicious of him sitting there like that and just then, a black Cadillac Escalade pulled up. Vulture-like, Mike circled the block, arriving back just behind the Caddy. He couldn't see through the dark tint but he knew this was the truck Sticks described. Mike clutched his pistol, calmed himself and maneuvered up beside it. Just like he figured, there was a woman behind the steering wheel but it wasn't her he wanted, then, the muscle-bound passenger came into view. In a split-second he took aim and pulled the trigger in rapid succession, letting the Heckler holler, until the clip was empty.

Click! Click! Click!

He pulled away from the murder scene doing 80, and turned onto Halsted. Never did he think a Chicago cop would have been staking out this block for its drug activity.

But there he was in an unmarked Chevy, lights flashing in the grill. Spent shell casings littered the truck's leather cabin. Mike floored it, running through traffic lights down a busy street. By now there were four cruisers in a hot and heated pursuit. Mike slung the pistol out the window, made a hard left, crashing head on into a Dodge truck, where the driver of it was fatally ejected through the windshield. His body smashed into another vehicle, decapitating the man. Mike snatched the driver's-side door open and galloped through the night on foot.

✳✳✳

Calvin had fled, sprinting down an alley. Camille had taken multiple shots to the face, neck and chest. While stumbling, Calvin paused to make sure he wasn't hit or being followed. Blood, skin and speckles of Camille's brain covered his shirt like lint. Rubbing his chest and abs, Calvin realized he was lucky. He only had a few scratches and cuts from the shards of glass that flew his way. He pulled out the bag of dope in his pants pocket, scooped some out with his fingernail and hit it. "Shit!"

Having escaped this night with his life, a couple grand and dope, Calvin knew it was time to let things cool down. In his trousers, with the butt end sticking up was his pistol. He knew it had a body on it too. But as long as it wasn't his. He couldn't go back to his mother's. That was a dead issue, having brought death to her doorstep, his second day home. "Fuck!" He could hear sirens and a helicopter. Calvin let the darkness of night blanket his path. He knew his mother would eventually find the coke he stashed in her pantry. He continued to walk high, angry and confused. He saw a CTA bus come to a complete stop for a crowd of passengers to exit or board. He jumped on that bus bound for downtown.

A part of Camille was with him, he rubbed her blood and flesh particles on his pants. "Rest in peace," he whispered to her spirit. He felt her presence and almost wished it was him that got hit up instead of her. He felt they should have died together somehow, yet he knew he'd cheated death.

The old woman sitting beside Calvin stood up and switched seats. She turned her nose up at him. He smelled like fish. Calvin didn't care. Flashing police lights now caught his attention out of the window. He lowered himself down, as to not be seen. There was a growing cluster of police vehicles all around the white Lexus truck. But the driver of it wasn't to be found. *Who was he?* There was two frenzied K9s barking like crazy, trying to follow a fleeing scent.

Calvin sighed. He brought to mind a solid ass white boy he'd met while in prison. His name was Nelson, from West Virginia. Nelson had always said there was plenty of money there. After getting off one bus, and on to another one, he decided to take what luck and dog food he had left to West Virginia. Having lost two women close to him in one day was a painful feeling. It was time for a vacation, an escape from Chicago's urban terror.

At the Greyhound bus station downtown, Calvin purchased a one-way ticket to the Mountain State, and nodded off until his bus departed.

Chapter 6

Deloris had a house crawling with question-asking police officers and homicide detectives. One was squatting down in her living room eyeballing a trail of blood drops. Her nerves were shot. She knew her house was clean, so she had no problem allowing them to search. Besides, they came shortly after with a search warrant. All they discovered was a box of bullet. The same kind used in the murder.

"Ma'am, since you have the bullets, where is the pistol at?" asked a clean-shaved detective.

"Sir, I don`t know. I don`t know how my truck ended up at a crime scene. And I do not know where my boyfriend is!" Deloris stomped her foot. "Will yall just please go now! Please!"

A seasoned homicide detective came forward, his beard white and his eyes cold as arctic ice. He studied Deloris. "Ms. Lane," he said. "This is a murder investigation. Where does Mike frequent? We know where he works, but we need to know?"

"No disrespect, but I'm done answering questions. I don't feel well. Just leave!"

While all of the law enforcement officers were leaving out, one said "we have your cell phone Ms. Lane. It was inside of the truck used in the crime. Pick it up down at the precinct." The detective handed her his card.

Deloris shut the door, then locked it. Using her house phone, she dialed up Momma. "Are you all okay? Where's Bri at?"

"We are thank God. I was calling you. Somebody tried to kill my son in a drive-by. A lady friend of his was gunned down in cold blood."

"The police has my phone," explained Deloris. "I had the home phone off the hook."

"I thank God my baby wasn't killed, he hasn't called, and I pray to the Lord he's alive. He was better off in jail. Lord have mercy."

The day's events had Deloris totally overwhelmed. She needed to vent to Momma. So much had to be expressed "We need to talk, can you come over?"

"Honey chil', my nerves is too wrung out to be out there driving tonight. Briana's asleep, anyhow. Worried about her father, as always. This chil' too young to be stressin' like this. I'll get out there tomorrow, or Sunday." Momma ended the call.

Deloris cried herself to sleep, she tried to unravel what just happened in her life. She awoke stricken by insomnia. She didn't know if Calvin was somewhere dead, and as it was, police were scouring the Southside in search of Mike. The thoughts of having to explain all of what she knew to Momma only increased her anxiety. Her truck was now impounded, and she was uncertain if it was safe to drive Mike's Lexus coupe. No telling who might be shooting at it. Sleep refused Deloris the luxury of avoiding her reality.

She called Pastor Scott, hoping he wasn't tied up with his overly-protective wife tonight. He answered. "Pastor Scott, can you come over tonight it's important."

"Where is Michael, sweetheart? Are you ok?"

"The cops are searching for him. They are saying he's involved in a murder. I'd rather talk in person."

"I'll pick you up. We'll go for a long drive and talk, or get a room. Is that okay?"

"Yes I don't wanna be here all alone tonight. Call me when you get close, I'll be waiting by the door."

***

Pastor Scott had known Deloris all her life. Her father was his right-hand-man in the dope game, until he got caught down in Texas with eight kilos, transporting them back to Chicago, half of that shipment was his. This was during the peak of the crack-cocaine epidemic. Police in Chicago were playing both sides of the fence. Higher-ups in the department got nervous, and to insure silence, he had to die. A dead man couldn't take the stand. On that sad day, Andre Scott exited the game, and found another hustle, religion. He was always there for Deloris in her times of need.

He pulled his new Bentley into the driveway and tooted the horn. Right away, Deloris came out, a classic-colored brown and tan Louis Vuitton in hand. She jumped inside and kissed him on the cheek. "Thanks for coming."

The sleek-shaped Bentley exited the interstate after an hour's ride. They got a nice suite where they wouldn't be found by anyone back in Chicago. After getting comfortable, and sharing a blunt, a few drinks, and affection, they laid across the bed and talked more in depth about Deloris' problems. Pastor Scott began to massage her shoulders.

"Pastor, I hate how he violated me like he did." She had already told him the story, twice.

The pastor scratched his bald head, and asked "What else?"

"I swear to God, it felt like he reached my soul. I never in my life melted like that before. My whole body gave in. It was one-thousand times better than any orgasm I ever had." Deloris began to cry. "My emotions are so fucked up."

Having been in the streets deep and done it all, Pastor Scott knew how to listen very well. Especially to what was not being verbalized. What she was explaining in a way, reminded him of a story one of his old whores had told him about. As he worked the kinks and tension out of Deloris' neck and shoulders, his mind took a long journey back some 30-years ago. His main, money-getting prostitute was named Mercy. A cold-blooded, long-legged, wide-bodied amazon. She somehow developed a deadly dope habit. Pastor Scott now recalled finding her body, stinking like a trash can full of skunks. She was bloated with rigor mortis in the basement of one of his whore houses.

"Damn, Pastor Scott. That feels so good," said Deloris. She scooted beneath his leg so that she could be spooned. This had been a cruel night. But at this moment, Pastor Scott was a blessing. But even so, his warm, tight embrace didn't take away her body's yearning for Calvin Jones.

***

It felt exhilarating leaving the murder capital, especially having escaped death. In a way, Calvin felt chosen, and yet, he felt his life had no purpose. And again, he was separated from Briana. He hit the tan-colored blow again, staring out the bus window into the black of night.

His unconscious hatred for women didn't remain back in Chicago. It followed Calvin straight to his destination. He couldn't wait to dog a stray bitch to death. Just like he'd done Deloris. He was sure she'd OD'd. He hit the heroin again. Nothing in the world took the pain away like it. Calvin nodded out.

Huntington, West Virginia was a world apart in comparison to the city. The sun was glowing, welcoming him into town. He stretched out. The air smelled fantastic. In front of the bus station, surveying the area is where Calvin stood. College girls donned in tight-fitting green and black attire flirted and waved at him. Calvin smiled. He waved back.

"Hi," said a thick, smiling brunette. She moved in closer and studied Calvin's prison tattoos. "Oh my God you're such a god." Her mouth fell wide open.

Calvin laughed. He'd never heard that line before "Am I?" he asked.

She undressed him with her big money-green eyes, and said nothing.

"Are you okay?" asked Calvin.

"I'm sorry. Can I give you my number? Just in case you ever need to release some stress." She smiled.

"That's cool." He liked her already. "What's your name shorty?"

"Treasure." She scribbled her number on a sheet of paper. "Here you go."

Calvin took the number and watched the bold young lady reunite with her giggling friends, all of them were well-built, and soon, the group headed down the street. Already he liked this new rural-looking town. It wasn't too much longer till a silver Navigator on 30-inch chrome pulled up. Calvin smiled. He'd seen pictures of this truck while in prison. He jumped inside. To his surprise, a white chick with strawberry-blonde hair sat behind the steering wheel.

"Nelson sent me to pick you up, I'm his sister, Jessie."

✳✳✳

Mike had come to terms that he had fucked his entire life up. He was now hiding out at one of Sticks' unrented properties. The floor was where he slept. My job's gone. My vehicle…Deloris, everything gone, he thought to himself. He had his freedom, but that felt to be jeopardized too, due to the fact that Sticks was suspect, and a scary dude. And he exposed himself too as the undercover snitch type, something he never could have fathomed.

Mike tried getting comfortable on the floor, yet hunger was getting the better of him. The rental unit had no heat, water or power. Suddenly his thoughts were disturbed. Sticks pulled into the carport and keyed himself inside. "Mike," he yelled. "I brought you some food."

Smiling, Mike came into view. The entire house was engulphed in darkness. "Thought you forgot about me, Sticks."

Sticks handed Mike a bag of KFC chicken. "I got you a prepaid phone too my guy." Sticks passed Mike the phone. "I know you'll need it."

"Thanks."

"So what are you going to do?"

Mike gave Sticks an uncertain frown before saying he didn't know. "I've got to get a hold of my girl, maybe..."

"Bro wait. Fuck that woman. It's over with. You're in this shit solely because of her!"

Mike broke down. The truth of the matter was difficult to digest. And the thought of it made him sick to the stomach. Literally. He vomited all over the garage floor. "I'll clean it up, Sticks."

Sticks had never seen Mike this way, ever. He didn't know what to say. But if his wife found Mike squatting here, it would get ugly. The cops, she would not hesitate to call. Sticks knew he couldn't imagine facing no harboring a fugitive charge. He sighed at the thought, watching Mike dial up a number in his new phone. He figured it was Deloris he was calling.

Chapter 7

One of the very first mistakes Calvin made in arriving to West Virginia was judging a book by its cover. Huntington was "jumpin'" like the big city when it came to the illegal drug trade. At least that's what Jessie told him. I didn't look like it from the outside. She drove Calvin to her house way out in the middle of nowhere. The whole ride she talked about how serious the opioid crisis was there.

Calvin got comfy on her sofa, surprised that Jessie loved rap music. She had been leaving and coming back all day. Back and forth. Calvin was street-smart, he easily equated her activities to picking up and dropping off.

Jessies's living room was neatly-situated, and clean. While relaxing on the couch Calvin nodded out, and didn't come to until Jessie and Nelson came through the front door together. Calvin stood up, "Good to see you!" He and Calvin dapped up.

"Damn it, dude, you've gotten big as a fucking tank." Nelson threw a few fake jabs at Calvin.

Calvin said "Thanks for lettin' me come to your world."

"Don't mention it," replied Nelson. "I'm actually glad you came down. I'm going to take you shopping dude, get you out of them rags."

They sat down beside one another. "I had to leave Chicago under some fucked up ass circumstances." Calvin glanced down at his blood-stained shirt. "Unfortunately there was some pistol-play involved. I lost a down ass bitch. So here I am, and I like it here." Calvin's eyes suddenly caught a quick glimpse of Jessie down the hallway wearing a pair of panties and bra. She disappeared into the bathroom and closed the door behind her. Calvin could now hear the shower running in the distance.

"I'm doing major things homie. Stay down here with me. I could seriously use a strong battle-tested lieutenant." Nelson sounded confident in his words. "I got this bitch on lock!"

"You know I'm down with the program." Calvin began to wonder where all this drug-dealing could be taking place. The lay of the land was expansive instead of concentrated. It felt weird.

"This is not the urban jungle anymore. I'm sure you noticed."

Calvin nodded. He admired the gold Gucci frames that set on Nelson's face. He was a different person than he was in prison. Or maybe in prison he was pretending to be someone else. Calvin's high was coming down, so he slumped forward. Both his elbows keeping him upright. "Yeah man, are there any projects or trap houses down here?"

"There's plenty of poor white trash down here." Nelson's face took a serious disposition. "You ever hear of carfentanil?"

"Never."

"It's an elephant sedative. The shit's one-hundred times more powerful than fentanyl, dude I'm the only person in the state distributing this shit in kilos." Nelson lit up a cigarette. "This drug isn't in the ghetto. But these hillbillies 'round here die for it, and die doing it. The demand for all opioids in West Virginia is through the fucking roof."

"Say less. I'm down." Calvin did not waste no time securing his position in the operation. At the same time, the hype he was putting on the elephant dope sounded like bullshit. Calvin knew fentanyl was knocking nigga's dicks in the dirt.

"Good" said Nelson. "That makes me happy. Welcome to Huntington, West Virginia. You'll be a millionaire in six months."

Calvin laughed, "When do I start?"

"You had any pussy since you been out bro?" asked Nelson.

"I had a little bit."

"You're gonna love it here."

Calvin thought about all the white girls he stood a chance of fucking. As of yet he had not seen a single black person. Just then, both their attention turned to Jessie. She struggled with a huge duffel bag, finally setting it at Nelson's feet. After tugging the leather bag closer, Calvin unzipped it, pulled the flap open and clutched his hands around two stacks of hundreds. That cash, he handed to Calvin. "Here bro. Jess's going to take you to get everything you'll need to get settled in and comfortable."

"Thanks Nelson."

"Don't mention it. I got an apartment for you. You got a cellphone?"

"Not yet," Calvin set the cash on his lap. "I'll get one while I'm out."

Jessie stood there in some black leggings, one hand on her hip. Her eyes studied Calvin's handsome features; his goatee and full lips. His powerful strong arms made her feel safe. And at this moment she knew exactly why Nelson needed him here too. Calvin would soon find out, she thought.

Nelson thumbed a text in his phone. Looked at his sister, "Jess, Calvin's my new lieutenant."

"No shit," she mumbled, then smiled.

Nelson wasn't in the mood for any joking around. "I don't want him selling shit. Transporting shit. I need him laser-focused on the security of the operation."

Jessie raked her fingers through her damp hair, and took a seat besides him. Her cell phone went off. "Nelson I got people waiting," she said focused on a text that just came in. Jessie swiped and thumbed the screen of the phone.

"Calvin she's going to drop you off at your apartment after taking you to the mall. I've gotta run. I'll call Jess's phone in about an hour," said Nelson. He hoisted the duffel bag up and headed for the door.

"Come on let's go Calvin," said Jessie. Outside, parked behind the house was a Toyota Camry. They pulled off in it. The ride to wherever they were going was a quiet one. "I've got to serve a couple people before we hit the mall, is that okay?"

"That's cool," replied Calvin, "what you serving out here?"

"Oxys. Roxys, heroin and we're pressing our own brand of pills too. Nelson doesn't want me selling. But I've got my own clientele, people I went to college with plus, I like to do my things too, ya know."

"Yeah, you fuck around, huh?" Calvin smiled. He hoped she did.

"I do. I use to run track, blew my knee out. Hurdles." Jessie pulled into a Walmart parking lot. "Pain killers got the best of me." She scanned the parking lot until she noticed another white girl walking barefooted toward the Toyota. "Pull that glove box open for me please, hun."

Calvin pulled the glove box open. He noticed a Glock, and a clear baggie stuffed with plenty of pills. By that time the woman without shoes on climbed into the backseat.

"Hey there, Jess." The woman's eyes were focused on Calvin. "Hello."

Calvin nodded.

"My goodness." The woman fanned her face with her hand. "My name's Amy Lee." She reached her hand out towards Calvin. Calvin shook it.

"Killa Cal," he said. "Nice meeting you."

"Here, Amy." Jessie handed her four pills, and took the one-hundred-dollar bill Amy pushed at her afterwards.

"Thanks Jess." Amy's eyes turned back to Calvin. "Is this your boyfriend, Jess?"

"He's a friend, why?"

Amy smiled. "Is it okay if I give him my number?"

"No," said Jessie.

"I'm sorry for asking. I was wanting to see if he...never mind."

Amy climbed out and headed towards the burgundy Challenger and pulled off.

Jessie fired up the Toyota and merged into the flow of traffic.

Calvin reclined his seat back, his mind bounced from Amy to Jess, both seemed to be angels, and this situation was literally too good to be true. Jess had a set of thick thighs, and a nice rack on her chest. She had some hips to actually balance out her lack of ass. She glanced over at him and grinned. "I wasn't about to let Amy lure you out to her house. She wouldn't be a good look for you." The shock of this new culture made Calvin take in a deep breath and shake his head. After a few more of the same style pill serves, they hit up a shopping mall, had lunch, and got better acquainted. Jess was the kind of woman Calvin had never dreamed about. Because her type, in his urban culture was so out of reach.

Deep down inside, Calvin told himself he would never go back to Chicago, except to see his mother and Bri. And of course to murder more people who betrayed him, who he felt was deserving of it.

Jess pulled up into an apartment complex called Rotary Gardens, situated behind the Walmart they'd stopped at earlier.

"Wow. Is this my new spot?" asked Calvin.

"Yeah." Jess killed the engine, and they carried all the shopping bags into a clean and cozy 2-bedroom apartment. "How ya like it?"

"I come from out the mud. I love it." Calvin had been smelling his musty armpits all damn day. "I'm ready to take a hot shower." Calvin stared into Jessie's eyes.

She blushed. She didn't know why she did. But it felt as if what he said was an invitation, subliminally, at least. As Calvin removed his shirt, revealing his chiseled chest and abs, her knees got weak. "I better go before I expose my weakness to you."

"You're funny, Jess."

"No I'm serious." Jessie spun on her heels heading to the door, and walked out. "I'll be back later." She shut the door.

The hot water felt amazing petting his body. Calvin took his thoughts to the night before. He couldn't believe Camille was gone. "I've got to call Mom's and Bri," he reminded himself at a whisper's tone. He lathered up again and froze, paralyzed in fear as the bathroom door slowly opened. It was Jessie. In her hand was the Glock. She aimed the pistol towards herself and set it on countertop. "Nelson called. He told me to leave this with you." Jessie's eyes slowly descended to determine if Calvin was packing. Her mouth came open in disbelief. "Damn."

"Thank you, Jessie."

Jessie leaned against the counter, overcome with curiosity and lust. "Thank Nelson. I know I'm going to."

Their eyes met. Her nipples began to jut outward, telltale signs that she was aroused. She rubbed the back of her neck and released a soft moan. With that, Jess turned and left.

Chapter 8

Deloris didn't have the heart to tell Momma what Calvin had done to her. They sat in the dining room drinking coffee. Briana found YouTube videos to watch, and in doing so it took her mind away from the shambles her young life was in.

They had been praying and discussing the deadly shooting, and the mysteries surrounding Calvin's disappearance. "His supervised release officer putting a warrant out for his arrest," said Momma. "He was 'posed to report."

"Did you call Cook County Hospital, Momma?"

"Yes, I pray to the Lord he wasn't kidnapped, and taken somewhere to be killed."

"Momma, stop. You're thinking the worse." Deloris clutched her stomach grimacing.

"What's wrong?"

Deloris said "cramps." She felt sick and sore. "I better go, my stomach acting up Momma." She focused on Briana, who sat on the living room sofa. "Get your things together

Bri, we're going home." The little girl sadly gathered her belongings.

Before Deloris could leave out, Momma's phone rang. She picked her phone up. "Must be bill collectors," she answered with "Who may I ask is calling?" Her face lit up with relief. "Thank God you called son. Thank you, Jesus." She covered her face with her hand to hide the falling tears from Deloris and Briana. "Are you okay. I've been worried sick about you and so has Deloris and Briana.

Calvin and his mother spoke for a couple of minutes then he spoke with his daughter. The whole while, Deloris squirmed in her seat. Briana looked over, pitifully handing her mother the phone.

"Daddy wanna talk to you." Deloris grabbed the phone and walked into the living room with it up to her ear. "Hello," she said.

"Delo, I'm surprised you are there I thought you would—"

"Who the fuck else is going to console you mother, you inconsiderate no-good…listen we need to talk. Where are you?"

"Nowhere close to Chicago."

"Where? I'll come get you, Calvin!"

"Now you wanna be sweet. What's up?" asked Calvin.

"Well. We just need to talk in person, I'm not mad anymore about what you did to me." Deloris gripped the side of her mid-section as her muscles continued to spasm. "I wanna apologize for how I mistreated while you was locked up. Calvin, baby please forgive me. I'm forever yours."

***

"I can't believe you got me out here like this following this woman. Man, you're bogus as hell," said Sticks.

Mike didn't reply. He just sat in the passenger's seat, keeping his eye on the backend of his Lexus LS 500. He hadn't been able to reach Deloris by phone so he resorted to some street investigative work. Sticks trailed by three car lengths behind Deloris. "I appreciate you Sticks." Mike wasn't sure if he hit his mark, he knew he'd blown the female's brains out. And was hoping that Calvin suffered the same fate. There were simply too many murders unsolved in the belly of Chicago's underworld, and Calvin knew in time, the cops would close the cold case.

"Where do you think she's going?" asked Sticks. He turned left.

"Looks like to the church she attends."

They parked at a distance, and from afar, they observed Deloris holding Briana's hand, tugging her into a church. Sticks glanced down at his watch. "Must be making funeral plans for her daughter's dad," said Sticks.

"I hope so."

Sticks shook his head. "Look, go jump in your car, pull off, and don't look back at that situation. Start over. Let her have everything."

"That sounds good. But my hearts too invested in this. I told you."

"Fuck that ghetto love bullshit! I wouldn't even be out here in the fucking slums right now, unless I was repossessing some low life's shit, motherfuck that bitch!"

"Watch your mouth Sticks. I don't disrespect that whale you got at home."

"You got some fucking nerve." Sticks frowned. "Whale? She's pregnant nigger!"

Mike turned towards his friend, smiled. "You're sensitive when it comes to that cave woman, aren't you?"

"Mike, you do what you gotta do, I'm running out of patience with you. You my dog. You love this bitch that just took a mule dick, so be with her. I've got to go."

Mike licked his lips, and built up the courage to bear the consequences of following his heart. He climbed out of Sticks' BMW, shut the door softly and stalked the Lexus, waiting for Deloris and Briana to emerge. Sticks vanished in the flow of traffic and was now only a blur. Mike moved in even closer.

By now, Mike leaned up against the LS 500. She had been inside for close to an hour, and still wasn't answering her cell phone. Suddenly, the front door of the church came open, and there she stood. The embrace she gave the pastor was odd, but Mike blew it off when Briana happily called out his name. She was all teeth, as her smile shined bright on the darkness of his mind. Pastor Scott locked the front door. He faded back inside, leaving Deloris to deal with Mike alone.

"Hey honey," said Mike to Briana. "How you doing?"

"Fine." She continued to glow.

Mike's eyes were red and probing. They were keen on reading Deloris' body language as she got closer, avoiding eye contact.

"Hey baby," said Deloris. "What are you doing…down here at the church?" She wrapped her arms around Mike, as did Briana.

"I'm here and that's all that matters, alright?"

"That's right. We need to talk Mike. The cops are looking for you for questioning. Why did you—"

Mike said, "Shhh!" He place a finger up to his lips. "Speak no evil, let's get in the car, and get out of town for a couple days."

They all got into the Lexus and pulled away from the curb. The whole time, Pastor Scott observed things from behind dark stained glass. He was a forward—thinker, with the street IQ of a real OG. In Pastor Scott was a wolf in sheep's clothing. He unsnapped his cell phone from his belt, glanced at the LCD screen a few times. And was able to tell exactly where Deloris was. He didn't give her the new watch for nothing and although he felt Mike was harmless, he knew Deloris was too precious to him to chance her safety. More than anything Pastor Scott knew Calvin Jones was the true threat, and if necessary, he would be dealt with. He headed into a mop closet and snatched a bucket, and mop. Waiting for him to clean up was a puddle of vomit. Deloris couldn't be pregnant, he thought, as the mop head sloshed through the purple bile.

Chapter 9

Calvin was standing out in front of his new apartment building waiting on Nelson to pull up. A barely-dressed, slim-thick milk-chocolate-complexioned prostitute sashayed up advertising her product and services. Calvin naturally found her attractive, except that she was pigeon-toed. "Shorty, you walking around here with that big ass hanging out, damn what's your name?" He gripped his crotch.

"Diamond." She grinned. "Wouldn't you like to have me for breakfast you sexy stud?"

Calvin squeezed his erection, her proper, country voice was an instant turn-on. "If I wasn't waiting on my ride, I'd love to start my day doing pushups in that pussy."

She giggled. "What's your name? I never seen you before?" Her eyes sparkled with desire.

"Killa Cal, shorty. I'm new 'round here."

Diamond shimmed up her leggings a bit causing the crease between her center to be so much more visible. "Well Killa, I'll be around. I'm out hunting for my morning fix, a girl get sick without it."

Calvin well-knew the sickness, he motioned for her to follow him into his apartment where he broke her off some dope. "That's just a down payment on some of that fat pussy. Get at me later."

The addict smiled, and said "Sure, Mr. muscles." She tucked the drug down into her bra and walked out, leaving her scent behind.

Nelson was out there in an extended cab pickup truck. Calvin jumped inside. The very first thing he noticed was the two young black dudes in the backseat. Both gave a silent 'what's up?' using a head nod. "The two in the back, they're my shooters, Misery and Dum Dum." Nelson backed the truck out and pulled off. "You strap, right?"

"Damn, right," said Calvin raising an eyebrow as the truck headed west.

"We had a small issue last night," said Nelson. "Three guys robbed one of my spots. We got intel on their location right now."

"Let's even the score then." Calvin's demeanor showed Nelson that he was indeed built for this lifestyle.

"Apparently they're asleep after a night of getting high and partying with my dope." Nelson pulled down his sunglasses, shielding his eyes. He turned left at a four-way street, and put his foot on the gas pedal hard.

"Local guys you know?" asked Calvin, considering the best method of execution.

"Out-of-towners. Georgia cats. We get a lot of that here. I'm having a hard time too with a notorious group of Detroiters, here thinking they're running shit."

Calvin knew how things went, he tapped Nelson on the thigh. "Pull over."

Nelson was about to ask why, but eased over to the shoulder of the road unquestioningly. Calvin stepped out. Pulled open the rear door, where he was met with a set of eyes searching for meaning. "Get in the front my nigga." The young dude did as he was told. Calvin got in the back. The truck pulled off. The dude he switched seats with wasn't right. And there was no way in hell Calvin was going to let that ride. His eyes were way too shifty. He wanted to see too much. He couldn't be trusted. A nigga wanting to see everything would be the same one telling everything.

They rode past Marshall University, made a few turns and ended up in some apartments. "This is Northcott projects."

"These aren't the kind of projects I'm use to but whatever let's handle this shit."

All four men headed toward an apartment where the door was cracked open. A pregnant white girl stood there looking afraid and as if she'd be delivering any moment. Nelson pointed her to his truck after snatching the cellphone from her hand. "Go sit on the tailgate." The woman did just that.

Inside the apartment a snoring light-skinned dude was awakened by a foot to the face. The other found a pistol shoved into his mouth. Nelson disarmed both men. "Yall boys thought you could steal my dope and get away with it, huh?" said Nelson.

The one with Ruger touching his tonsils shook his head side to side. "Eh, em, didn't do it, 'e did it!" he tried to say. Calvin pulled the other man upright then he split his face open with his Glock. He pistol-whipped him again. Wham!

"He did it!" Calvin cracked him once more. "Auggh!"

"Let's get this over," said Calvin, he pulled a pillow off the sofa, put it over the man's face, and pulled the trigger. Poof! Poof! Poof! The dying man's feet trembled as he expired there.

"Please!" said the dead man's partner. Crack! His head was met with the butt-end of Calvin's pistol.

Crack! Then again. "Hey, tell me where you from?"

"Atlanta, Georgia!" Blood covered his face entirely. But that did not absolve him of his trespasses.

"You wanna go back to Atlanta, young nigga? Huh?"

"Yes I do. We only came here to make some money."

"Alright. I'ma let you go back. Okay?" said Calvin.

The young dude motioned vehemently, "Yes! Yes!"

"Can you fly? Because the wings I'm about to give you, you'll have to fly back down South. Have a safe trip!"

To muffle the explosion, Calvin gave him three to the head, using a pillow as a silencer. "Let's go," he said. Everyone rushed toward the door in a hurry just like he expected. Nelson was the first out. The other two left the back of their heads exposed. Calvin raised his pistol. Boc! Boc! Both men crashed into the door frame, half-hanging out of the apartment. Calvin pulled them both back completely inside, and closed the door behind him on the way out. He didn't draw suspicion by running, but the gun, he tucked it. Instead of getting in the front seat with Nelson, Calvin got in the back. Nelson eased out of the projects slow and cautiously.

"Oh my God. I heard gunfire back there," said the woman expecting a baby.

"Boo, no you didn't." Calvin chuckled. "Those were firecrackers I let off."

"I frickin' hope so." She cradled her unborn and Calvin could easily see her baby doing flips. "You got my dope for me Nelson, my reward I was promised?"

Before Nelson could respond, Calvin said "Homebody, take us to my place. I'll reward shorty real good."

"Thanks."

"Ain't nothing." Calvin ran his hand across her thighs. She wore a purple skirt and he realized just then that besides not having shoes on, she had on no panties.

"That feels good," she whispered, feeling three of his fingers penetrating her. She opened her thighs wider.

"I never had white pussy before."

"Oh really," she said, her eyes closing. "I'm going to orgasm. And I get crazy wet…when…I…do."

Nelson pulled into the apartment complex and sat there, parked, as Calvin and Krissy went into the apartment. Backing out Nelson noticed the puddle on his back seat.

He didn't really know how to accept the fact that Calvin had just killed two opps, and two of his own men, in his presence. One thing for certain, he was satisfied to the fullest with Calvin's murder game. Some niggas talk about it, Calvin was about it, thought Nelson.

***

Calvin had taken a strange fascination with the pregnant woman. She told him her name was Kris. He lied, telling her his name was Fifty Cent. She was ready to get high, bad. "Please Fifty Cents, this baby in my stomach is gonna beat himself totally free if he don't get no dope." She scratched her belly. "We're both opioid addicts."

Calvin returned to the living room with the heroin, his shirt off and only in a pair of boxers. She raised up her skirt. Resting more on her side, so that she'd be comfortable. In anticipation of getting high Krissy's unborn started moving around. "Mommy about to give it to you baby, be patient."

On his knees, Calvin moved in closer. Krissy was beautiful, soft, and warm. He didn't know how to handle a white woman. His adoration for white women developed in prison, and now he had a driving hunger. His penis was fully erect. Just the sight of her laying there so sweet and innocent, and submissive had his dick throbbing and seeping pre-cum. She pulled her butt cheeks apart. Her vagina was hairy, and yet perfect.

"Daddy come on. You act like you wanna make love to me."

Calvin actually did, and found it utterly surprising that she detected it. "I do," he whispered in her ear. "I really do."

"Well get me high!"

He scooped up a bump with is fingernail. "Hit it, but go easy its strong."

She hit the dust. Calvin hit about the same amount, then removed his boxers.

"My God I've never seen a cock so huge. You think it'll fit? With me being eight months, you're gonna be giving my poor baby a beating."

She couldn't take her eyes off of Calvin's manhood. She took a hold of it softly. Then she guided it into her mouth. Caressing her face, he could now see the ghost she was about to become today. "Can I make you forever mine Krissy?"

With Calvin's thick black inches stretching her mouth wide, she rocked her head up and down, seductively. He pulled out her mouth, but she kept a hand around it, slow-stroking his cock, squeezing it until veins rippled across it. "Fuck me with this big black dick Fifty Cents."

"You like that dope dick?"

"Yes." She batted her eyelashes at him.

Calvin reached for his dope, pinched out some of it and sprinkled his erection from head to base. "Snort some off of this hard motherfucker, Krissy." She did. Calvin maneuvered out both her breasts, exposing gigantic areolas and pink long nipples. Her stomach was shaped like the moon. A full one. Her nipples leaked milk.

"I'm afraid," she confessed. "Go slow, I'm scared." Before she could nod off, Calvin pushed the length of himself deep inside her. "Oouch, Fifty Cents. B'easy. I'm shallow and very narrow, daddy."

Calvin pumped lovemaking-slow. Krissy resembled the movie star, Kate Winslet, except she was quickly turning blue; the speed of his thrusts increased, as her body trembled and released into the afterworld. "Forever mine?" asked Calvin, finally ejaculating in her womb. Her blue eyes stared at him, unresponsively. The windows to her soul reflected an emptiness. Calvin then carried her body into the bathroom, and placed Krissy into the bathtub, after which he set out on foot to Walmart for an ax, and trash bags. Calvin thumbed in Nelson's number, Nelson picked up right away.

"You all good, Cal?" asked Nelson.

"How about doing me a favor."

"Anything. What's up?"

"How about coming by and giving my female friend a ride home in about an hour?"

Nelson got silent. "Ohh, I'll be there."

Chapter 10

Mike, Deloris and Briana had taken the few hours' drive from Chicago up to Wisconsin Dells, a resort area, where they rented a nice Four-Star suite. By now, Briana was sound asleep on the sofa, her tablet still aglow.

Mike and Deloris got comfortable and wanted to discuss things more freely. Briana took in every word anybody ever spoke, and in this, Calvin had figured out the location of their home. "I can't believe I missed that monster," shouted Mike. He took a swallow of his drink, then rattled the ice cubes around in the glass.

"Honestly Mike, I'm not feeling the shit you did. I'm just gonna keep it frank." Her hands moved in a motion as she spoke that proved just how fed up she was. "An innocent woman died, and you are the killer!"

Mike smacked Deloris to the floor. "This shit's your fault. You fucked my life up."

Deloris staggered to her feet, holding the side of her face. "I know you just didn't put your god damn hands on me!" She charged him with the fury of a mad bull. She gave him lefts, rights, lefts to no effect. Each punch came, he bobbed and weaved, until he finally yoked her up by the neck and tackled her to the bed. "You fuckin' stop it, stop!"

Her struggle to break free was futile. His physical strength won, but his emotional side showed its weakness. Tears fell, many of them. "I'm struggling to get over the fact he violated your body. Your body belongs to me. How am I supposed to feel about touching you intimately ever again?"

"We'll get through this," said Deloris. "We got to pray on it."

"Deloris, be one-hundred. Don't lie. Did you willingly have sex with him?"

She looked Mike square in the eyes. "No. I put that on my life!"

"Did you enjoy it?" Mike situated himself to better read her response. And her reply didn't come timely. "Did you?" he asked again.

Deloris pulled him closer, "He raped me Mike! Who enjoys being raped?"

✳✳✳

Jessie shook Calvin's shoulder, "Wake up, Cal." He jumped out of his nod, scanning his surroundings. "Nelson had to run out to Kentucky and sent me to come see you."

Jess noticed the ax on the sofa hanging from the opening of the Walmart shopping bag. "Calvin." She smiled. "Not to sound like a racist or anything but I've never met a black guy who uses. Are you high?"

The way her head moved as she spoke, and her searching eyes caused Calvin to turn away in shame. "I use here and there. Not every day." He placed a hand on his face.

Jess twisted her lips. Raked her hair, and surveyed the situation.

"A girl overdosed, before I nodded out I was about to dismember her body. I don't know what to do. Maybe you can help me dispose of her?"

"Where is she?"

Calvin stood up, and Jess followed him into the bathroom, "Oh God, no Krissy Jenkins!" Jess covered her privates by pulling her skirt down. "We have to move the body. I've got a plastic tarp out in the car. I will go get it."

They were able to get Krissy's blue body situated behind Walmart, and there, is where they left her laying. Her years of opioid addiction was now over. Jess and Calvin headed to her place for the night.

Jess flicked on the TV and kicked off her Pumas. Calvin sat beside her. That's when a local news story began to air about the four slain men earlier, and the missing woman whose apartment they were found in. "Police believe the murders were drug-related," said a news reporter. Jessie turned the tube off. Calvin noticed a sex toy in between the cushions of the sofa. Seeing Calvin looking at it caused her to notice it too. Jess blushed, pulled it up. "Say hello to my little boyfriend." They both shared a laugh. "Hell, a bitch single, and saving this good snatch for Mr. Right."

Calvin felt awesome being in West Virginia. He pulled out his bag off dog food. And as always, Calvin sent it up both nostrils. Jess smiled. She reached out for the bag and did the same. Together, right beside one another, their heads dangled lifelessly. Jess's cellphone rang incessantly. She summoned herself back from the depths of ecstasy to answer it. By now Calvin's head fell into her lap. "Hello?"

"Jess!" said the caller in a panic. "Jess! Somebody put a hole in Nelson's head. His body was just found in his car, and the shooter placed a Detroit Lions cap on his head, I guess to make a statement! Where can we meet up?"

It didn't seem real, not tonight. It all had to be a nightmare. Jess dropped the phone as her head bobbled, straining to stay upright.

"Jessie! Jessie," screamed the caller into the phone. The line when dead.

***

Pacing back and forth while in his home-office, Pastor Scott had activated the microphone on the watch Deloris was wearing. He was resorting back to his old criminal ways. Something, he knew and felt was about to happen. He overheard Mike delivering a blow to Deloris' face and for that lapse in self-control, it was going to cost Mike dearly. He sat in his black leather chair behind his desk and removed the wireless headset from around his head. He had heard more than enough.

He sat there for a long while completely immersed in his thoughts. He rubbed the goosebumps away that spread across his arms, and continued to meditate. Murder was inevitable, premeditated murder. Pastor Scott slid one of the drawers out on his desk and searched with his hand until he found the .45 caliber he kept there. He unzipped his briefcase and set the pistol inside.

It was getting late, Pastor Scott had church in the morning. He stood up, stretching his cracking joints. Before retiring for the night, he put the headset back on and logged in to his Spy app. And what filled his ears was the sounds of bodies clapping together, panting and moaning. This went on and on and on. The angry pastor removed the headset from his head, but not the idea of eliminating Mike from existence. That idea would incubate overnight, hatch by morning and be executed by nightfall.

Before crawling in bed with his wife of 34-years, Pastor Scott said his prayers. He asked his Creator for forgiveness in advance.

Chapter 11

Calvin held Jess in his arms, helping to make her feel that everything would be fine. "It's going to be ok. He'll pull through," said Calvin. "He's strong."

"Thank God," it just grazed the side of his head, and went out of his shoulder. Jess pointed her finger on Calvin's back. "It came out right here."

While Jess was at the hospital throughout the night Calvin stayed at her house. He felt at home there, but as it seemed, Nelson's operation was sloppily-run and unorganized. "What was he doing, delivering some weight and got jacked?"

"Well," said Jess, sitting down. "He had been having conflict with two guys out of Detroit named Streets and Nephew. Those two and others were extorting him, or robbing our street-level dealers."

Calvin sat down and put his arm around her. "Where are the assault rifles? And do you know where these Detroit niggas be at?"

Jess pulled Calvin's arm down the hallway and into her bedroom. She lifted the mattress. Laying there was two AK-47s and six 30-round magazines. "Grab 'em," she said.

"Yeah this what I need." Calvin pulled the AKs off the box spring, as well as the banana clips. "You know how to use these?"

"I'm a country girl of course I do." She grabbed one of the rifles, then jammed in a magazine and aimed the weapon at the alarm clock on her nightstand. She tossed the chopper on the bed. "Baby, I'm drained. I need a shower and a nap." Jess sat on her bed kicking her shoes off. "My life sucks right now." She pulled off her shirt, then her pants. "I'll be back."

While Jess showered Calvin gave thought to things. Chicago was on his mind. He hadn't been there no time at all, and his body count was already halfway to ten.

Jess came out in a white silky robe, and you could tell she was stressed, and needed some release therapy.

"So the way things look now, I might be going back to Chicago, Jess."

"I figured that." She pushed out her bottom lip. Next Jess crossed her arms across her breast. "Cal, can I pay you to help me get situated before you leave? I don't know what I'm going to do with my life, much less Nelson's operation."

"What do you need me to do?" He placed a hand on her thigh.

"What don't I need you to do is the real question." Jess guided his hand further up her thigh. She put it right on her vagina, and pushed one of his fingers between her sticky wet folds. "I wanna get choked. Smacked, fucked hard. I want my hair pulled, ass totally bored out, cunt ate. Can you—" Before she could finish laying out her demands a boom! came kicking at the front door, but it didn't come open. Boom!

Calvin dove to the floor, gripping the AK47, and Jess clutched the other one. She sent a round into the chamber like a soldier on the battlefield and let it rip! The door came wide open. The first two coming inside instantly found multiple holes in their chest. The third invader got low, unleashing cannon-sized slugs. Calvin had never fired a fully-automatic-style weapon until now. The masked man with the chrome Desert Eagle jerked and twisted, his body being torn apart. Jess didn't run from the front door, she ran out, stepping over the three bodies, firing at the Monte Carlo trying to flee the scene. The windows of the Chevy shattered, and the driver's head went crashing into the dashboard from the six slugs that diced through it. The vehicle veered off the road into a ditch and flipped over half a dozen times.

Calvin withdrew the empty magazine, and jammed in another one. He crawled over to the dead, removing their handguns from their hands.

Jess, she extended her hand out to Calvin, pulling him to his feet. "You hit?" she asked. Her eyes examined him for damage, her naked body beneath the robe fully exposed.

"I'm good, you?"

"I'm all right. Take my car go to your apartment. I'll be there as soon as I get this shit dealt with. Don't even think about going back to Chicago, not without me." Jess stood up on her tip-toes, her lips pursed waiting for a kiss. "Good shooting! Now get out of here. Hurry up." She spun a key off her key ring and handed it to him, after he kissed her. "Hurry up."

Calvin set the rifle on the passenger seat, fired up the vehicle and took off. Upon arriving at his apartment, he found Diamond at his doorstep. Her eyes sparkled with desire, again.

"Hey muscles. Told you I'd be back." Diamond smiled. "You got anymore dope?" she asked.

***

God is in charge of the storm!" yelled Pastor Scott. The church was jam-packed. Hands clapped.

"Preach!" someone in the back roared.

"No matter what you've done, repent. You can't hide from God. I pray all God's children obey and repent! Stop what you're doing. Repent! Do it now!" He danced around. "Repent!"

Deloris had arrived late with Briana. She left Mike at the downtown suite they'd rented in the heart of Chicago. She enjoyed the getaway. Mike was now making arrangements for a moving company to pack and move their belongings into a huge 5-bedroom home out in the south suburbs. After all Deloris had gone through recently, she needed the Word in her life. She pulled Briana closer by her side and listened carefully to the message Pastor Scott was preaching.

He was in a midnight-blue suit, sweating, hollering, and dancing all about. He had the older ladies fanning themselves. "We're being tested everyday! Satan will lure you. Uh! Do you wrong! Uh! But when that happens, uh and it will happen! Uh. You got to stand strong! Uh! Stand on the Word. Uh! Stand on it!" The pastor wiped his face free of tears and perspiration and smiled when he saw Deloris and Briana. He held his arms high above his head toward the heavens. "Resisting the desire for repayin' evil for evil is man's most difficult problem in this world...." He went at it for an hour straight. "You've gotta put ya pride to the side at times, and return good for evil."

After service ended, Deloris, with Briana in tow worked her way through the crowd towards her pastor. She had never felt so many men rubbing against her butt in her life. She ignored it. She shook his hand for the sake of appearances. His wife turned up her nose at Deloris, and twisted her lips at Briana, then the witch walked off with Sister Johnson.

"Pastor, I just wanted to let you know I'm back in town, and still without my phone. I'm gettin' another one later. I'll text you. I'm moving. I'll text you the address too, okay?"

"Baby, you do that." He came in closer into her ear. "If that no-good nigga ever put his hands on you, you pick up something and go across his head."

Deloris' eyes grew wide. She showed her signature smile. Then she gave the man a hug, as did Briana. Deloris couldn't believe how much Briana was starting to look like Pastor Scott.

"Check your Cash app, later," he whispered. "I've got to shoot move." Pastor Scott walked off socializing with the congregation.

Deloris pulled the Lexus away from the curb, feeling rejuvenated. Mike took care of her body and Pastor Scott calmed her spirit. Her mind turned to Calvin, and she smiled. As she got closer to the suite, Deloris noticed Briana had fallen asleep in the backseat. What she saw next brought tears to her eyes.

Mike was being led to an undercover-looking vehicle in handcuffs. In yellow lettering, on the backs of the cops' shirt read ATF. Deloris put the car in 'Park' climbed out and click-clacked up in her heels. "Why—"

"Get back ma'am!" The agent whipped out his pistol and pointed it at Deloris. "I'll put your brains all over this sidewalk if you don't get the fuck away!"

Her feet froze, as did her heart. Mike's eyes were both swollen shut. Deloris covered her mouth, using a hand. Mike was tossed inside the unmarked vehicle. He said 'I love you.' She read his lips. Before she could say the same the car speed off.

***

Jessie struggled carrying the full 10-gallon gas can from the garage into her house. She made up her mind that the three dead men would burn tonight. As would her old boring life here in West Virginia. Quickly Jess doused the bodies thoroughly, and onto the sofa, electronics, her bed. She had already taken out what was most important to her, and put it in the Navigator. It was well over a million in cash, which was just a fraction of cash she had access to. For now, it would be enough to give her and Calvin a good start together in the Windy City. She brought enough drugs as well. One of her greatest fears of all was being without and dope sick.

Standing outside her home, Jess took in a deep breath. "This is it," she struck a wooden match and flicked it at the long trail of gasoline, snaking through the front door. The flame engulphed the house in less than a minute. Once in the truck, Jess turned on some rock and roll, she turned it up as loud as it could go. She knew that would drown out the inner voice of reason. Calvin's apartment is where she headed straight to.

Calvin took a while coming to the door, and when he finally did, he struggled incredibly to keep his head up. His eyes were low, and bloodshot. "I see you've started the party without me." Jess rested her hands on her hips. "Smells like sex in here. Did I interrupt something?"

She pushed him out of her way; he staggered backwards, pointing her attention to the bathroom. "Some bitch overdosed on the dick. I put her in the tub."

Jess, stood there paralyzed with shock. The woman's naked body sat there, eyes blank, aimed at nothing. Her mouth hung open, wide. "That's Diamond. Her street name's Brown Sugar. My God." Jess got on her knees searching for a pulse. "She's gone. How much did she do?"

Calvin shrugged his muscular shoulders.

"Why's she naked and semen's dripping from her vagina? I guess you don't know that either." Jess examined the tracks along the prostitute's arms and legs. "I hope you used a condom. Did you?"

Shaking his head up and down, Calvin lied. He was as high as a motherfucker. Diamond had given him a Xanax just before he gave her the dope dick she had been dying to receive.

"Forever mine," mumbled Calvin waving at Diamond.

Jess pulled him by the arm into the living room. She pushed him on to the sofa, and began to pack up what little things he had, along with her AK-47. Before leaving out, she went to see Diamond for the final time. She once was the prettiest girl on the varsity track team, Jess found a sheet and out of respect, she covered her nakedness. Over the past year, Jess herself was responsible for fifty-one overdose deaths.

Shame was scribbled all over Calvin's face. Jess was walking his way. "Let's go!" she ordered, snapping her finger. Her voice reminded him of one of the correctional officers back at the prison. Calvin rose to his feet. Jess grabbed the chopper, and the plastic bag with his things. "We're headed to Chicago." They walked out into the night.

Tonight, the moon was full, Calvin looked up at it, and let out a howl so loud it startled the shit out of Jess. It was time for a change. She eased her curvy body behind the steering wheel. "Baby get your fine chocolate ass in here!"

Calvin got into the cabin of the SUV and as bad as he hated to admit it to himself, he was madly in love with Jess. She didn't judge him for his faults, and a bond, they developed, although an unusual one. Jess fiddled around with the music, then hit a button to activate the 6, 15-inch subs in the rear. She backed out, and floored the Lincoln.

Chapter 12

The ebbing of the tide caused the houseboat to sway from side to side. This was causing sea sickness, and the brutal beating Mike was taking wasn't feeling nearly as bad as it had when it started. The two men pretending to be federal agents had tied his hands high above his head around the inner structure of the boat. He had been stripped naked. Mike was sure that his ribs were shattered, and his kidney ruptured. He was pissing blood, and clenched his teeth, as the larger of the two delivered eight consecutive thuds into Mike's midsection.

Beneath Mike's feet was a large sheet of thick clear plastic covered with urine, and feces. Strengthless, Mike's head drooped, blood oozed from his nose and mouth and ass. "Please, no more."

"Your turn, "said the larger man. He wiped the blood from his fist with a towel.

Mike had heard the smaller of the men call the larger one "Creeper." The smaller man's wrist ached. He massaged his fingers, grimacing as he did. "I've got a much better idea." The smaller man, drenched with perspiration walked off and returned with a whip.

Creeper smiled.

"Only the strong shall survive," whispered Mike, motivating himself to stay alive. He was actually thinking it and the words poured out, along with more blood.

"Hell you say?" The small man slowly unfurled the black leather bullwhip.

"Nothing," moaned Mike, "I ain't say nothing. Why yall doing this?" Mike knew that Lake Michigan stretched the distance of twenty-two thousand, four-hundred square miles, and at this point he wished to be thrown overboard. The whipping he knew was to follow would break him in every way. The restraints on his wrists were unmercifully tight and cut off his circulation of blood flow. The first crack of the whip across the back felt like a strike from a lightning bolt. It sounded like the clap of thunder. "Auuughhh shit!" Mike shut his eyes. He braced his soul to absorb to be next blow, and it came just as fast. Pow!

"My turn!" said Creeper, yanking the whip from his partner's grip. "You pissed off some powerful people boy," growled Creeper. He raised the whip, sending it forward with all of his might. Crack! The impact left a deep raw groove in Mike's flesh. Mike yanked, cried, bled, trembled.

"Kill me," he begged. "Please! Kill me."

***

Pastor Scott had just disconnected his call with Deloris, and felt guilty. He scratched his head and considered deeply if he should allow Mike to live or die. Clearly Deloris loved him and he loved her. And if she forgave him for putting his hands on her, he figured he would to. Pastor Scott hated to hear Deloris so distraught like she was. No matter how hard he tried over the years to inspire her to be independent, it never worked.

Pastor Scott's crime partner back then, Deloris' father had done a good job of spoiling her. And he picked up right where he left off. In every man who dated her, she sought that father-figure, and all she wanted to be was daddy's girl. He sighed, thinking of the good old days, while sitting in his Bentley. On the seat beside him sat his worn leather bible. He flipped through a few pages, finding his favorite scripture. It was highlighted in orange, after donning his reading glasses, he read the verse and let the words settle in his heart. He softly closed the bible. Then called his two long-time hit men, Creeper and Saint. Nobody answered. It might be too late, he thought. He dialed again.

***

The big man's cold fingers lifted Mike's face to see if he was still alive. He was barely breathing, if at all. Through the slits of Mike's swollen eyes he studied the interior of the sailing vessel they were in. No doubt about it, this was a life-or-death situation. And death was slowly swallowing him up.

Mike's perspiring hands had long lubricated the tightness of the ropes that held him in place. In a grotesque way, his back was torn apart, literally. It was as if every nerve was exposed and ablaze. Mike begged for the angels of death to take him away.

The Rambo knife not too far across from him held his attention the entire time he was being tortured. He was certain this was in retaliation for the woman he murdered the other day. His captors were exhausted, one held his nose tight, the stench of feces, urine and blood combined was way too much to bear on this balmy night. The air was thin, and moisture covered Creeper's imposing body like a blanket. The small guy's cellphone vibrated. He answered. It was Pastor Scott. "Pastor. He's about a thousandth of an inch from the hell that awaits him. Shall we—"

Mike wiggled free, lunged for the knife, clutched it, and in one smooth stroke, he plunged it completely in the man's neck, blood gushed out close to six feet, sending him crumbling to the floor in shock.

The small guy smartly dropped the cellphone and made an attempt to climb up the short stairwell to the deck. Mike snatched him down, and immobilized him with a karate chop to the base of his skull. Then he worked him into a punishing cobra clutch. The stranglehold sealed off any and all oxygen to Saint's brain. Mike tightened it as hard as he could, now hearing the man's neck pop in three different places. "Ahhhhhhhuuuughhh!!!!" screamed Mike, the veins in his neck and arms rippling tight. He could feel no pain, only the relief of the small man expiring in his very arms. Mike pushed the lifeless corpse onto the sheet of plastic, where the man laid stiff in the foul mess.

Catching his breath, his chest heaving, Mike picked up the phone. The person on the other end rudely ended the call. He thumbed in Sticks' number as best he could through his slither of vision.

"Hello?" answered Sticks.

"Homeboy, how soon can you get down to the lakefront? Lake Michigan. Please I need you please!"

"I'm downtown now! Where are you?"

"On a boat in the lake somewhere."

"What?" asked Sticks. There's a bunch of fuckin' boats on the lake fool."

***

Fear paralyzed him to his bed. His wounds painful. Engrossed in sadness and anger, combined with despair is how Nelson felt. The 10 o'clock nightly news had just aired an alarming segment, showing Jessie's home having been engulphed in flames. What was left was only smoldering black ashes.

"Charred human remains were discovered in this home." A female news reporter pointed the cameraman's attention to a flatbed low truck in the distance. "And nearby police found a dead man from Baltimore, shot to death in an overturned vehicle. His identity is being withheld until…" The news reporter rambled on and on, and to Nelson, the vehicle looked all too familiar to him. "The FBI and ATF has been on the scene investigating. They say its drug-related."

Nelson aimed the remote at the TV, turning the screen pitch black. His wife, Sharon hadn't even bothered to come up to the hospital to see if he was still alive or not. He closed his heavy eyelids, picturing the two explosions that placed him here today. Nelson's back ached. He sat now on the edge of the bed, his teeth gritting as he was bearing the pain of standing up. He took a baby step, what startled him was the hard and sudden knocking at the door. He sat back down, his goal of leaving the hospital tonight was thwarted. Two homicide detectives came inside. Neither looked friendly. He had either seen them on TV or read about their work many times. "I don't wanna answer any questions not without my lawyer!" said Nelson clearly and loud.

One of the detectives moved in closer, he walked slow and with a limp. His light-grey dog-like eyes studied Nelson. He cracked his knuckles. "But I didn't come to ask you any damn questions punk." A very confident smile began to crease itself across the fedora hat-wearing detective's face. "I just wanted to inform you that ATF found bodies at your sister's. Dead bodies. We're unsure if any were her. Have a good night."

Before the detectives could walk out, the other turned around, he and Nelson made direct eye contact. The 17-year veteran saw the fear.

"What?" asked Nelson. "Leave!"

"I sure'd like to take this fuckin' badge off an' break your fuckin' face in you opioid-selling piece of shit!" The detective headed directly toward Nelson. "You're killing your own blue-collared people out there, pushing that poison shit dumb motherfucker!" The fed-up detective lifted his hand back about to slap Nelson across the room, but his cool-headed partner caught his arm in mid-flight.

"No. Not now, Detective Hunt." He held the overly-emotional detective's shoulder as tight as he could. "C'mon. Let's go."

"Oh," said the detective, "I almost blanked out." He frowned, wanting nothing more than to wrap his massive hands around Nelson's neck. In spite of being restrained by his partner, he met Nelson's nose with his very own. "Tonight, my young pregnant niece was found dumped behind a Walmart, dead of an opioid overdose! And I know in my Appalachian heart your dope is what did it to her!" The detective gripped both his fists around Nelson's hospital gown, yanking him tightly, closer.

Nelson's pathetic attempts to squirm free were unavailing. He swallowed the lump of guilt in his throat, and prayed they didn't have an arrest warrant forthcoming.

"You've drawn first blood punk! But at the end of my investigation, I'm going to nail your nigger-loving ass to the cross! I hate them black bastards didn't kill you dead!"

"Let's go," said the other detective, tugging at his arm.

The room door came swinging wide open. Standing there was a bow-legged, tight mini-skirt-wearing, caramel-complexioned Jamaican woman with flowing jet-black hair and juicy lips covered with red lipstick.

"If ya don't get your dirty got dam hands off my husband, I swear fore God, I'ma fuck ya up!" She kicked off her Red Bottoms, and unzipped her Chanel handbag, rifling her hand down inside.

Nelson's eye, although red grew wide as cue balls. Both detectives calmly walked out. Sharon flew over to console Nelson, embracing him. She smelled like one of the expensive perfumes she owned. "Are you fine? They didn't hurt you, right too bad?"

Nelson shrugged his shoulder. More than anything, his pride was hurt. "I'm good," he said.

"Two of the spots in Northcott projects got robbed tonight. Detroit niggas. I know it had to be."

Nelson sighed.

"I got a call from Jess."

"You did? How...where's she?" Nelson exhaled a gust of relief. "Tell me she's okay?"

Sharon pulled his hands in hers, then noticed his Rolex was gone, as was his jewelry. "She's on her way to Chicago in the Navigator with your new enforcer...friend."

Nelson gave thought to the entire situation. Everything else Sharon was saying only bounced off his eardrums. Shit had never been more real than it was now. Attacks were coming in from all angles. Jess was the last remaining blood-relative he had left in West Virginia, aside from his cousin Mia. And she was in the process of moving to South Carolina. Jess was the sweetest, and closest thing to his heart, he trusted her more than his wife. And even though Jess had an addiction he stood by her side through it all. Never did she need to sell her body to avoid dope sickness.

Never did Nelson imagine his drug operation would take off like it did so fast. Nor did he think Jess would take off so suddenly, either. But that's life, he thought. He knew Jess had always been deprived of love, and raped for years by their perverted uncle during her pre-teen years. Nelson erased the slow-trickling tear off his face, and tried to drift his way back to the moment. Sharon's full lips were flapping up and down, so Nelson tuned his heart into her word. He loved her Jamaican accent.

"I'm worried. I don't feel safe at the house alone without you baby. I'd rather sleep here with you baby. I love you honey." Sharon sat beside Nelson and softly pulled him into the warmth of her breast, and cradled his stressed and wounded head.

"I love you too," he cooed. "But we're leaving here." As bad as he hated to raise up off Sharon's two pillows, he knew it was required. "I've got to check my traps," he said. They kissed. "I got too much cash in the streets."

***

The long, winding and rutted roads stretched and twisted like a heart's arteries through the hills and valleys of West Virginia, the very place where the opioid epidemic began.

Sharon handled her showroom-new 2021 Mercedes sports utility vehicle with class, cutting through the dead of night like a hot knife through butter. Along the ride, Nelson tried constantly to reach Jess by phone, but could not. His calls went straight to her voicemail. He set Sharon's phone down in a cup holder. Then pointed, "turn here. Slow down." This was Sharon's first-time way out here in isolated Appalachia. She was nervous.

Before them now was a towering 16-foot chain-liked fence that was covered with seemingly never-ending spirals of razor wire that span well into the darkness, "Wait here." Nelson eased slowly out of the Benz truck, still in his hospital-issued gown. Sharon killed the engine and headlights. Then she pulled up the heavy .44 automatic beneath her seat and rested it on her lap. The cold steel gave her the chills.

Nelson carefully punched in a 10-digit security code into a portal, and the imposing gate slowly slid open, just enough to allow him in. Then it shut closed. Glowing from the building was candescent lightening. That's the way Nelson walked.

Inside, it was dark. Nothing looked or felt out of place. Nelson headed into a small musty cell where he flicked on a light. Lined neatly across the wall were six brand new pill presses. He moved fast toward an adjacent room. In the room, darkness was present and a medicine-like stench that turned his stomach. He leaned against a wall, trying not to spill his guts. Nelson hit the light. It was all there. "Shit," he whispered. A single box was missing. Stacked neatly were tan-colored boxes. Each box had Nike's logo across the side. Nelson did another count, but the math didn't change a bit.

Inside these boxes weren't gym shoes, but carfentanil. A salt-shaker sprinkle amount of this dope could easily knock an elephant down to its knees. No longer would opioid addicts have to trek up the Heroin Highway to urban jungles in Baltimore, the cash would stay in the state. On one of the large boxes was a note, Nelson dreaded the missing 10-pound box, even though 49 boxes sat there. His bowels ached, he felt nauseous from the odor of the drug. The only person who could have taken the box was Jess. Nelson noticed her handwriting the second he unfolded the note.

"Bro, I'm headed to the Windy City with our new lieutenant. There, I'll open up a new market. I pray for your safety here in West Virginia. But it's time to expand, and devise an exit plan. I am bringing with me enough cash to settle down and be comfortable. With elephant treats, I'll be fine. I promise to finally get clean and detox. I want to make you proud of me. I am not going to be your junkie sister anymore. You'll see. I Promise. I love you, Jess."

With his heart beating like that of a black college band's drum on football Saturday, he placed the note up to his heart. Before their mother passed, he'd promised her he would keep Jess safe. Over the years he had managed to hold up to his promise. But the unruly demon he was at war with and in partnership with was growing stronger by the day. And all the money he had stashed now couldn't take the excruciating pain away. Ironically his best-selling product was originally a painkiller. "Poor Jessie," he whispered.

Lightheaded, Nelson let out a groan while climbing up into the Benz. The leather smell drowned out the scent of Sharon's perfume. "Is that Burberry you're wearing?" he asked, trying to camouflage his emotional wounds.

"No, it's Chanel, baby." She backed out cautiously, easily able to sense his agony inside.

Nelson sighed. It had been a long day. It's not every day a man gets grazed by a headshot, he figured.

"Where are we going, home?" asked Sharon, her hand now caressively touching Nelson's thigh. "Let's get a room somewhere."

"We're going to Chicago sugar, you ever been there?"

"Never."

"Neither have I," he said. "But I've got to catch Jess. I got a bad feeling." Nelson closed his eyes visualizing the worse. Praying for the best. Hoping somewhere in the middle their fate would fall.

"We do need a getaway." Sharon put the large caliber automatic back underneath her seat and continued driving through the dark mountains and hollows of West Virginia.

Chapter 13

Calvin could tell Jess longed for urban adventure by the way her big beautiful eyes dazzled at the Chicago skyline as they drew closer and closer. She deactivated the Navigator's cruise control and followed Calvin's instructions that guided them to a downtown plush high-rise suite.

During the ride here they had gotten more acquainted on a deeper level. Both of them feeling as if they had hit jackpot in meeting the other. Both had revealed missing pieces and secrets of their pasts and vowed to be a couple, and journey the eternity of life together.

In the luxury suite together, all alone, is when it all seemed so surreal. Jess unfastened the large duffle bag and made it storm in the best way ever. Over a million dollars in one-hundred-dollar bills covered the suite's carpet and bed. Bills clung to the bottoms of her feet as she headed to the twenty-sixth-floor balcony. "God, this view takes my breath away." In the horizon, the Sears Tower caught her attention next, it was the tallest building in the sky.

Calvin couldn't take his eyes off of the money. He'd never seen so much of it at one time. Jess sashayed back inside and took a firm hold of his arm. "Is it official, for real?" She ran her hands and eyes across Calvin's powerful chest and broad shoulders. "Don't play with my emotions." She did away with his shirt, all the while feeling on his body like a sculptress.

"It's definitely official, Jess."

"Do I belong to you?"

Her eyes begged him for honesty. "Every bit of you belongs to me," he assured her. Their lips connected, and their tongues united and welcomed the magnificent bond now forming between them. Calvin's hand explored her soft willing body. He removed her sweats, then her pink panties, finally pulling off her skirt and bra that hid her mouth-filling 42 DDs. His tongue slow-circled both her erect pink nipples. Her knee began to get weaker.

Calvin lifted her up and carried her into the marbled shower where he set the mountain-raised beauty on her two feet. After undressing himself he joined her.

Jess was enjoying the foreplay. "I'm so fuckin hot," she whispered. The warm water pelted their bodies, causing steam to rise like clouds. Calvin's tight-gripping hands worked the muscles of her round ass. At the same time he sucked his name on her neck, leaving behind long-lasting purple passion marks. She panted, moaned. "I've got to feel your huge cock in my throat," she cooed. "Fuck my face with that black dick!"

"Jess eased to her knees while using a steady hand to jack Calvin's massive erection. She opened wide, inserting his penis into her mouth. Gripping his thighs, Jess pulled him in deeper, coaxing him along so he would give it to her how she loved it. She smacked his ass cheeks a few hard times until he finally caught on to what she desired of him. Submissively, she said. "Make me suck it all."

She knew there was no way in hell all of his dick would fit. But sheer country girl determination got her damn close. Jess slid his length completely out, catching her breath. She was proud of herself. Next she smacked her face with it. It didn't seem real, it was too good to be true. Plus the moans of pleasure Calvin was making turned her on even more. Jess pulled it back in her mouth and fingered herself.

By her hair, Calvin lifted her face up. "You ready to feel this big pathfinder stretch that tight pussy?" He turned the shower off.

With her head bouncing up and down, she said "I want it in my ass first okay?"

She pulled him by his erection into the room and pushed him down onto the pile of cash. Using two fingers, Jess primed her corn hole. After climbing on the bed, she squatted above his erection. She took in a deep breath, frowned in pleasure while stuffing him in a fourth of the way. "You're hung like a horse, ouch daddy." Her strong thighs powered her body up and down. Jess purred, twisting herself and gyrating. "Make me take it. Make me!"

Her ass was so tight it hurt. Calvin clenched his teeth, his hand gripping Jessie's breast. No woman had ever done him this way.

"Make me!" she cooed, and bounced, her mouth seeping saliva. "Ouch, daddy. It feels good." She took one hand and methodically worked it across her clit, fast. "Watch this."

She bounced faster. "Watch," she cried, her own eyes now focused on her clit too. Calvin's precious dick was sending shock waves through her body. She trembled. "Watch it cream, for you daddy." Her soaked hand strummed even faster. "You seeee it? Look!"

Jess was in the throes of an anal orgasm and a vaginal climax at the same time. Her threshold for pain didn't exist. Thick cream began to run down and puddle on Calvin's stomach. "You see it?" Her hand didn't stop. She trembled more, using her sweet cream as lubrication. "See what black cock can do to me?" She was out of breath. Calvin, although still in her ass could feel the thumping contractions of her vagina. "Who owns this big black cock?" She reached behind her waist, pulling her cheeks apart. "Who motherfucker!" Tell me now!?" Jess pinched both his nipples as hard as she could. Then twisted them. "Answer me!"

"Ah, shit ouch!"

"Is this my cock?"

"Yeah! Shit, it's yours, Jess."

Jess's thighs were on fire. She jumped off of his patient and unselfish candy stick, spit on it, and guided it in her mouth.

"You nasty bitch," moaned Calvin.

Jess popped it out her mouth, "You love nasty bitches like me. Don't you?" She went back to sucking away. After coming up for air she said, "Can you handle a woman like me?"

"No question," he replied. "Once I hit, ain't no other nigga gone know what to do wit' it."

Her hair was wet, and her jaws ached but she wouldn't stop until his semen flowed into her belly. "I know what you want," she said, pulling her hair back. "I came four times," she added. "I love you."

With all of the passion in the world, she kissed him. She eased off the bed with one-hundred-dollar bills pasted all over her perspiring ivory-colored body. With the near-empty bag of heroin they'd been snorting, she headed for his erection.

"Wait," said Calvin, "Not so much."

"Shut up." Jess powdered his chocolate dick, kissed the mushroom-shaped head of it. She carefully scooped him out a bump with her fingernail and put it up to his nose, "You wanna give me that dope dick don't you big daddy?" Jess used two fingers to pull her pussy lips apart. Then she finger-fucked herself. "I'm tight."

Calvin rolled around and separated her thighs further open. Her vagina had a wet lustered shine. He kissed his fortune cookie. Then pushed half his length inside her.

She pulled her thighs fully open for him. "Make love to me now, daddy go slow, slow and hard," said Jess feeling the mighty euphoria that tingled up her spine. Her breathing intensified.

Calvin pumped her slow and deep, she felt like the blessing she was. "Forever mine," he whispered in her ear.

She whispered it back.

Chapter 14

More than a dozen federal and state authorities had Sticks and his wife Mary in their living room in handcuffs. "Don't cry please sweetheart," he told her. Sticks could also hear his children crying in the background as officers tried to calm them down. He sighed. "My wife's fucking pregnant. Will you take the damn cuffs off her? I'll tell you everything!"

Sticks had a bad vibe about helping Mike last night. He had been cutting his front lawn when the unmarked cop cars swarmed his home like angry bees. An officer had tackled him while on his brand-new riding lawn mower. His head ached. His heart ached.

Officers huddled in the kitchen, then uncuffed Mary. She massaged her wrists before hugging their children. Together they sniffled and tried to wrap their heads around what was going on.

"Stand up," said an agent tugging Sticks by the arm, leading him into his master bedroom. "Now sit down." He sat. "Tell us what you were doing down on Lake Michigan last night?" The agent held a digital recorder up to his face. Six other eager-for-information officers stood anxiously around the ransacked bedroom. Sticks paused.

"Spill your guts boy, or you're being charged with two counts of Capital Murder," yelled a red-faced tobacco-chewing state cop.

Stick coughed. "This bullshit all began a few days ago. A guy came home from prison."

***

Deloris whipped Mike's Lexus into the packed church parking lot just beside Pastor Scott's Bentley. She slung her purse around her shoulder and high-stepped it toward the running vehicle and jumped inside. Pastor Scott pulled off in a hurry. He was on the phone with someone and held up a 'be quiet' finger at her. Then he veered onto the expressway. Beads of sweat formed like fallen drops of rain across his forehead. "I can't talk right now, let me call you back." He tossed the cellphone over his shoulder onto the backseat. "Fuck!" He pounded the steering wheel. "Fuck!"

Deloris jumped. "Pastor, I got here as soon as I could. I haven't even unpacked yet. And I dropped Bri off at Momma's."

He ran a hand across his face, removing the stress puddles. Then he cooled the vehicle's cabin off by fidgeting with the AC controls. "Your boyfriend, car salesman killed a couple guys with mob ties last night."

Deloris aimed her eyes at him, "what?" She covered her mouth, "Mike?"

"Yeah." He merged the sleek vehicle into a growing line of stopped cars at a toll booth. He punched it, after paying the toll, signaled and reduced his speed. "And they're demanding to be reimbursed for their loses. Forty-eight hours."

Deloris rolled her neck and eyes. "What that got to do with you?"

Pastor Scott didn't bother to answer her, certain things about life and the underworld he lived in were simply too complex to explain to an outsider in detail. He was glad to be in position to help her, but as always, her burdens became his. He reclined his seat back, loosed his tie up, and kept the nose of the Flying Spur headed south. "You know what I always need from you when I'm stressed out like this."

She dug down in her purse and pulled up a bottled water, unscrewed the cap and took a swig. She reached over and unzipped his pants, releasing his semi-hard member. Then she wrapped her lips around it. Up and down her head went, catching the attention of highway travelers. They finally pulled into their favorite trysting place. Using the back of her hand, Deloris wiped her mouth.

Pastor Scott handed his pretty young thing a couple large bills. "Keep the change."

While she was renting the room, he situated his penis back where it was. Yet he couldn't stop thinking of how costly of a day yesterday was. He glanced at his Bell & Ross timepiece. Time definitely wasn't on his side right now, but Deloris was. And he had a couple million-dollars worth All State life insurance on her. In his heart, he didn't want it to come to that, but right now, time dictated his agenda. And it would forever be money over bitches.

He pulled out his black lamb skin driving gloves, tucked them into his briefcase right along with his favorite pistol. Just then, his eyes caught a glimpse of a black man suspiciously moving in his direction up in the rearview mirror. He knew he was paranoid, and more than likely tripping. He was just given his deadline, he still had plenty of his time left, so he figured.

Deloris came out, just as sexy as always, seductively smiling. Pastor Scott adored her and felt bad about his need to give her a one-way trip to be beneath the wings of the Almighty. Horror stopped her dead in her tracks. The masked gunman she was witnessing aimed a pistol. And he left it explode. She screamed.

Boom! Boom! Boom!

The Bentley's driver's side glass window shattered in the aftermath, as did the pastor's face. Deloris screeched, but she shut up quick when the pistol turned on her. The ski-masked gunman yanked her by her weave and dragged her ass to an awaiting white van. He pushed Deloris inside, climbed in and handcuffed her to the base of the rear-row seats. After that, two sharp blows to her head lulled her deep into the valley of darkness.

"Stupid ass, dick suckin bitch!" said the furious pistol-carrying man. He slammed the van's door shut. Then he hurriedly climbed behind the steering wheel and mashed out.

***

They knew they had to move swift and with tact. Law enforcement officers had all of the info they now needed. Thanks to the Sticks. Two agents stayed with Sticks and his family to ensure no warning call would be made to their perp. The others headed over to the rental property where Sticks had taken Mike last night. SWAT had also been radioed and was en route, along with a helicopter.

Within 30-minutes, the law surrounded the home, guns drawn, no search warrant was required. Yelling officers sent the burgundy-colored front door crashing down and stormed inside. They were anticipating a fierce full-blown gun battle, or a suicide-by-cop. They came up empty-handed. Mike was long gone.

What the cops found were blood-soaked bandages and the cellphone of one the deceased men from the boat. Although this was crucial evidence, there was nothing more. Several of the officers began to leave.

Across the street, a two-story brick home's front door hung wide open. But it was nothing unusual for this predominately white, upper-class neighborhood, expect for the Golden Retriever that barked incessantly and spun in the circles. The K9 charged toward the officers, stopped, then did a complete three-hundred-and-sixty-degree spin, pointing their attention to the brick house.

The men of law enforcement, including one woman withdrew their sidearms and cautiously followed the K9's lead. Inside the home, suffering from a single bullet wound to the center of his forehead was an old white man. Beside him, his wife laid crumpled in a pool of blood, handcuffed to her soulmate. She was alive, and conscious.

"Ma'am, are you okay?" asked one of the officers, realizing she was blind. Other officers searched her home for the killer.

"I think I'll be okay," said the old woman. "My husband, I think he's dead." The well-trained dog sat beside the woman, avoiding the lake of blood on the carpet. "There, uh, wasa…you got to uh, excuse me. I'm somewhat incoherent. A negro broke in, demanded cash, and the keys to our van."

Paramedics soon arrived, and this affluent community was now crawling with the angry police. A cold-blooded murderer was on the lam. One of the officers clutched his radio in hand, "I need an APB on an all-white Dodge van, blue pin-striped, Illinois plate number 8946F!"

***

Jess was the golden key that unlocked a new world to Calvin, and it was blowing his mind. To see white privilege, up close, and personal gave him a broader perspective of how he fit into the grand scheme of things. He'd sent Jess to go rent them an exclusive 4-bedroom condo way out near the Chicago Bears training facility, in Lake Forest, Illinois; Northeast of the city, a safe distance away from all the inner-city madness.

Next, Jess bought him a triple-black pre-owned Hummer. He'd always wanted one. And now, it was a reality, not a fantasy. They spent the afternoon, kissing, holding hands, spending paper, shopping, and falling even deeper into the web of love.

"How do I look?" asked Jess.

"Delicious, boo."

Jess felt awesome in the Gucci, and designer wear. She couldn't believe how much of a movie star she looked like. Especially in her Cartier sunglasses. With the new phone she'd purchased earlier, she went selfie crazy, puckering her lips, slithering out her tongue for the camera. "My first day of sobriety!" she posted, with the hash tag #GucciBitch.

As the ghetto dwellers took to the streets when the sun went down, out of habit, Calvin found himself doing the same. He chose Gucci too, an all-black sweat suit to compliment his H2. They were completely out of dope, and beginning to both feel sick.

Jess rubbed her stomach that started to spasm. "I'm not feeling too well," she confessed. She still hadn't taken her Cartiers off. They hide the dope sickness evident in her eyes. "I need it, bad," she whispered.

Chapter 15

By the time Mike pulled near the church parking lot, he spotted his Lexus where Deloris had parked it earlier. He slowed the van down, and yet, as it seemed, the sad news about the pastor's demise had already reached the ears of his congregation. "Will you shut the fuck up Deloris so I can think!" yelled Mike toward the back of the van.

Deloris was in tears; in agony, in the vice grips of fear and distress, and she had two goose eggs sitting on her forehead.

Pulling her out of the van. In the midst of so many church-attending eyewitnesses would not be wise. But Mike knew he had to dump the hot ass van, "Baby why? Why?" she said. "Why's you doin' me like this?"

Mike wanted to pull over and beat the living shit out of her, but for logic's sake he played it like an iceberg. He pulled the stolen van into a vacant lot next to the church; walked around and violently slid open the door of the van. One of her heels was missing and she tried to kick Mike in the face. He deflected the attempts. "Look at you now, you slut bucket ass whore! The whole time you been fuckin' and suckin', and with the holy-rollin' pastor huh?"

She cried even harder. "I'm so sorry!"

"Yeah, stinkin' bitch. That you are. I gave you everything and anything and because of it, it makes me a weak nigga?"

No amicable reply came.

Mike ripped her cute skirt completely off of her. It was one he'd purchased for her. Then he smacked her across the face so hard it sounded like a stick of dynamite went off. "You scream, and it'll be the last thing you will ever do!"

"Pleease, Mike." She shuddered.

Using her skirt, he leaned in and stuffed her mouth with it, and with brute strength, he stretched it around her head. "I ought to strangle you!"

Her screams had been muted to perfection. She squirmed, moaned but would not be able to liberate herself alone. "I saw you suckin' dick. You have been fuckin' too, ain't you? You ho ass nut bag! I was faithful to you!" In one powerful yank, he snatched off her thong. He studied her vagina, then he realized that the mourning crowd in the church parking lot had thinned out. He reached in the van for his pistol, slid a slug in the chamber and gave serious thought about jamming the barrel up her vagina. "Bitch you literally fucked up my life." He pushed her legs wide, and knew then…it was the pussy. She had thoroughly pussy-whipped him.

Now, moving in the direction of his Lexus, Mike's ears tuned into a set of squeaking brake pads. His heart raced, his intuition told him who it was, and his killer instincts did the rest.

Two uniformed cops pulled up behind the van, and Mike trotted in their direction, dumping a barrage of hot lead. The black cop's hat flipped off, as did the upper portion of his skull. The officer crashed to the earth, his roof now missing. The white cop moved like a cat, and crawled behind the police cruiser. "Drop your weapon!"

"Drop yours!" screamed Mike.

Mike's bullets were sending sparks, and fragmented bits of mental across the cop's face. The cop cradled the trigger of his Glock, wanting nothing more than to put multiple holes in this gunman. He knew he was almost out of rounds, and waited with poise and courage. He raised up over the hood of the bullet-riddled police car, pulled the trigger, and missed. Mike's final bullet ripped through the cop's fingers and tore a big hole through his neck.

The white cop fought for life placing a useless hand over the bullet's entrance. He stared up at the sky, fading away; the clouds moved slow. Then there was Mike's shadow above him. Then Mike's black angry face. Mike picked up the cop's police-issued pistol. Took easy aim, and squeezed the trigger. "That's for George Floyd, and Trayvon, bitch!"

Boc! Boc! Boc!

With the pistol in hand Mike stormed into the van, his hands trembling like crazy, uncuffing Deloris from beneath the seat. He took a tight fist full of her hair and marched her to the side of the Lexus, half-naked. After it was all said and done, Mike sped off, less than a mile away he shot pass a state trooper doing close to one-twenty, easy. A chase ensued.

***

It was not but a few minutes later, when Calvin parked in front of his mother's apartment building. He felt naked without his pistol, and knew he had a bench warrant out for his arrest. "Bae, I want you to meet my mother."

Jess forced a smile. "How special." She leaned over and kissed him, her hand touching his crotch. "You giving me my dope dick tonight." She stroked the length of this penis slow.

"I thought you said the pussy was tender earlier?"

"It is," she said, "can't you tell how I've been walking today?"

Inside, there was nothing but love. Calvin's mother welcomed his new woman, as did Briana. Briana played in Jess's hair the whole time. Jess's cellphone chimed as Briana crawled all over her, giving her hugs. Jess noticed her brother's comment to her earlier post. She giggled, then Nelson's face filled up the screen of her phone. "Who is that?" asked Briana.

"My brother," she said. "Hey bro!"

"Jess, what's up? I guess you're all Gucci'd up, looking too good for West Virginia, and your brother." Nelson laughed. "You look happy, Sis." Nelson saw the face of the young girl. "Who is that cute little one?"

"She's Calvin's little princess. I'm in Chicago, safely. You got my letter?"

"I did. Please. Please, Jess. Be..."

"Bro, chill, I'm fine. I know my limit."

"That stuff ain't to be—"

"Where are you?" asked Jess, cutting him off. "And I haven't used any of it."

"Why he got a boo-boo on his head?" asked Briana, pointing at Nelson's face on the phone.

Jess laughed up a storm. "He hurt himself, " said Jess to Briana.

"Sis, I'm in Chicago." He aimed the phone at Sharon. She waved. "Hey Jessie, girl. Let's go shoppin' in the morning."

Calvin chopped it up with Nelson and gave them the address to the condo, so they could link up tomorrow. They indeed had much to discuss. Calvin hoped to get his blessings to be with Jess. But if he didn't, fuck him, he thought. She wasn't going nowhere.

Calvin noticed Jess clutching her stomach, so he kissed his daughter and mother goodnight, and pulled Jess by the hand. They walked out into the darkness. Cars bumpin' loud music raced up and down 117th Street. Like lovebirds, they walked hand in hand. Looking into Jess's innocent eyes made Calvin come to terms with some things. Prison, he would never go back to, death he would accept before another stretch behind bars. They say money couldn't buy loyalty, but in this case, it must have been untrue, he considered.

"What are you smiling about?" asked Jess.

"Just thinking about you baby. I haven't been this happy in a while."

"I feel sick." Her face twisted. "Dope sick."

They reached a house that was dark, where a long line of black men and women stood. To Jess, they all looked poorly cared-for. And one woman held a crying baby. In the murky shadows stood two men, hoodied-up with dreads. One of the men brandished a chrome pole at his waistline. From a slit in an open window, on the side of the house another dealer inside the house received the cash in exchange for the blow. In awe, Jess simply stood in her Gucci gear, shocked by such an open-aired drug operation. Calvin pushed seven one-hundred-dollar bills into the opening of the window, and out came his dope.

"Keep movin'," said the man with the pistol at his waist. "Thanks for shoppin' wit' us dog."

Calvin put an arm around his woman, and they walked back the way they came.

"Hey you?" called a female addict.

Calvin turned around. Through the darkness he tried to make out her face. "Whuddup doe?" he said, studying her features.

"Man, ain't you Brenda's son?" she asked, scratching her ashen skin.

"Yeah, why?"

"I'm fucked up. Sick is fuck. Pussy ain't sellin' t'night. You 'member, back when you was a youngin' an' dem boys jumped you and took your shoes?"

Calvin's mind traveled back to that exact point in time. "Yeah, I was like ten-years old." Where this junkie was going with this conversation he didn't know.

"You 'member, huh?" The woman offered a grin, minus a dozen teeth. She scratched her neck. "I'm the bitch who gave you that Saturday Night Special. Your first gun."

Calvin smiled, he pulled the skinny woman into an embrace. He didn't care that she was filthy. She once was a brick-house, with a hypnotizing walk. He undone the wrapper on one of the bundles and hit the lady's hand.

"Thanks," said the junkie. "You sure grown up."

Jess smiled, the gesture touched her heart. "I'm Jessie. Everybody calls me Jess." They shook hands.

"Follow us," said Calvin. He led the way as the ladies chit-chatted. They all got up into the truck. Calvin looked over his shoulder at the woman, after pulling out the small amount of carfentanil he'd packaged up that morning. He was afraid to sample it and so was Jess. Calvin set it in her palm, just as softly as she'd done the Saturday Night Special way back then. "Put this out on the block, and let a nigga know what it do. You may need to cut that bitch first."

"Cool." She smiled." Thank you." Then she eased out, headed toward the alley.

Jess used her teeth to rip open one of the packages, careful not to spill any. Before snorting some herself, she used her fingernail and scooped out Calvin some. He leaned in. He hit it. Jess did the same. They looked at one another just to be sure the other one was there. Calvin fired up the

Hummer. He fought to keep his head from crashing into the steering wheel. It was a losing battle.

There was commotion, then someone snatching at the door latches. Suddenly, a small hand landed with a thud, twice against the tinted glass. "Daddy! We gotta go pick my Momma up!" yelled Briana, in tears. She hit the window again.

Calvin's mother screamed "Calvin!" which killed his nod. Jess hit the switch unlocking the doors, and she and Briana climbed up into the backseat.

"What's going on?" said Calvin.

"Deloris is in the hospital. We got to go pick her up. Her boyfriend killed Pastor Scott!"

Calvin pulled away from the curb. As they drove, Momma had Deloris on the phone consoling her. "Thank God you're alive."

Chapter 16

"The shooting lasted forever!" cried Deloris. She hugged Briana tight. "I never knew that man was crazy." Tears flowed non-stop down her face.

The little girl sat silently in the backseat beside her mother, clearly traumatized for life. Above Deloris' eye sat a criss-crossing track of black stitches, and lumps.

"Well," said Momma. "I just don't get it." She knew there was more to the story than what was being said. She gazed out into the night trying to solve the puzzle. She sighed. "You can stay at my place as long as you need."

"Thank you, Momma."

Calvin pointed out the directions from the passenger side, as Jess pushed the big truck through the city. He couldn't wait to get home. At the same time his heart went out to his daughter. As far as Deloris, he knew the sexy thick white girl behind the steering wheel was taunting her trifling ass. The fucked-up way she did him while in the joint was a pain he'd never forget. And the shit she'd gone through today wasn't nearly as treacherous as what he wanted to do to her. At a stoplight, Calvin leaned over and grabbed Jess's face.

He pushed his tongue in her mouth, and didn't stop kissing her until his mother yelled his name. The light had turned green, and Jess turned red.

Briana looked at her mom for her reaction. She liked Jess. Jess looked like her Barbie doll.

Furious, Deloris shut her eyelids to the bullshit, and brought to mind the horrendous events of the past few days. She felt Briana's little arms go around her tightly. "I love you Bri," she whispered.

"I love you too, Mommy."

They arrived at the apartment. In the distance, fire trucks, police and ambulances littered the shoulder of the street. Nothing unusual for Chicago, the city where murder is as common as a cough. Deloris, Momma, and Bri faded into the night, all headed into the apartment.

"Let me walk them up," said Calvin. He caressed Jess's thigh, then followed behind the ladies of his life.

Jess locked the doors.

Calvin didn't go completely inside. He softly pulled Deloris by the wrist before she crossed the threshold of the front door. He pulled her deep into his strong embrace. And held her for a long while as she cried. "Are you done fuckin' with them lames now?"

He gripped a firm handful of her ass in his palms, because he knew that was her weak spot. She responded with a moan, "Forever mine, Deloris never forget that. I own you."

Deloris yanked away and shut the door in his face. Then locked it. Deloris sat on the sofa in the dark, still uncertain if

Mike had gotten caught by now, or even killed. She said her prayers, hoping he was dead.

Outside, a crowd formed and moved zombie-like toward the Hummer. Jess's head rested on the glass, as if it were a pillow, her face turning blue. Her eyelids shut.

"Aye!" Calvin galloped their way. He kept his hands in the pocket of his sweat suit, faking like he was strapped. This used to be his block. "Whuddup doe?" he said.

It was the woman who gave him his first gun. "Little brother," she said. Her words came out frantically. "This shit put two bitches down tonight." She smiled. "The news will travel fast. I got them young niggas up the block on my line. I need more of this shit, they want weight. You still straight?"

"Naw, tomorrow be out here tomorrow night. What they call you?"

"You ain't know, I'm Angel. "

"Did you try it?"

She shook her head, "Crack's my thing. I'll fuck with the dog but it's a nasty bitch when you can't get it."

Calvin smacked the window of the truck where Jess was, he couldn't wait to get her home. Being out this late at night was something he would not do often. Jess climbed into the passenger seat. Her ass all in his face, he could small her pussy.

"Hey," yelled Angel. "What you call that dope? What brand?"

"Dope Dick."

Jess looked over at Calvin, her eyes aglow with lust and fire. "That's what I need." Jess blew him a kiss. "Dope Dick."

Chapter 17

"... It's like each and every thrust, when you're on top sends me closer to the kingdom of heaven, and I'm just floating there at the gates, in total peace, and one with you and the universe." Jess planted a wet kiss on Calvin's chest. "Does that make any sense?"

They had both just awakened from an eventful night of sex and drugs at their new empty condo. On a pallet of comforters piled on the bedroom floor, they cuddled, and kissed. What a night, Jess thought. Her hand moved across his abs down into the forest of his pubic hairs. Today was about to be yet another day of addiction battles, and hopefully some progress.

Calvin was still drifting to the moment, and gave thought to what Jess just said. "With me it feels the same, seeing your sexy ass body go numb, and you're creaming and squirting, trembling. I love that, I love killin' the pussy." By now, he was fully erect.

Jess shivered. The gruesome images of those two women in the bathtub flashed in her mind. She was beginning to understand his fetish of weaponizing his penis by lacing it with heroin. It felt so good, but brought her so close to death. Too close. She took his manhood far into her mouth.

Just then, the doorbell rang. She kissed the head of his penis and peered out of the venetian blinds. "It's our furniture delivery." Jess clapped her hands, while Calvin pointed her attention to the large oval-shaped wet spot on the comforter. Jess blushed. "You make me ejaculate like a water fountain."

The doorbell rang again.

After all of the leather, brass and glass was delivered and set up, Nelson and Sharon arrived. Uber Eats brought them all breakfast. Once Calvin and Jess showered together, Calvin and Nelson took to the streets.

In anticipation of shopping, Jess grabbed about fifty-grand from the closet. She and Sharon had plans to shop till they dropped downtown.

Nelson still had his head bandages on. But now he had a Chicago White Sox baseball cap covering it. They were riding hard in Calvin's Hummer, and Nelson said "Dude you put any of that Cardi B out yet?"

"Cardi B?"

"That shit bro. Jess helped herself to a whole box of my shit, sayin' she was going to open up some new markets here. If she's not careful she'll be opening up a fed case or her own coffin."

"She's good," said Calvin. "She not doing no hand-to-hand transactions. Shit, all l want Jess to do is count the money and get it to you so we can keep sticking and movin'." Calvin turned left. "I'd like to open up a detail shop and a music studio. Shit l envisioned while in prison."

Nelson nodded. "Look I don't want no money or drugs, or even my sister to ever come between us. So I'm going to be blunt. Jess has a habit."

"Who doesn't," said Calvin. "In one way or another, we all do."

"Yeah. But l mean a serious, expensive opioid-addiction habit. Try four or five-grand a week, and to compound that, she's algophobic."

"What that mean?"

"She has an abnormal dread of pain," said Nelson. "Been like that since childhood."

Calvin wasn't trying to hear that shit, as far he could tell, Jess loved pain. If he only knew, thought Calvin. "Well pain is nothing she'll need to fear with me."

"I've been supporting her needs, letting her do her so she could stack her bread up. Dude, she's all I got. If you're going to be with Jess, don't abuse her. You got a solid and trustworthy woman on your team."

"Trust me," said Calvin. "I saw what she was about when some niggas tried to rob her. Kicked the door in."

"Say less." Nelson fired up a Newport after smacking one out the pack. "I'm going to miss her. So I guess I'll be making trips here often."

"Respect." Calvin stared Nelson in the eye. "You a real motherfucker Nelson, on my Momma. I fucks with you the long way. But one thing."

"And what's that?"

"No, two."

"What's on your mind, champ?" Nelson matched his playful grin.

"One, the shit's called 'Dope Dick', not Cardi B, my guy. That name's whack as fuck."

Nelson laughed.

Calvin snatched Nelson's White Sox cap off his head, then tossed it out the window. "We rock the Chicago Cubs on this side of town. You can't be up here set -trippin'."

He pulled the truck to a slow creep beside Angel who was standing out near a crowd. Nelson looked on, fascinated by the dense urban jungle.

Nelson started doing some math in his head and quickly realized then, the astounding profits there was to be made in Chicago. They could do numbers that would make congress faint. His attention was shifted to the female who jumped into the back of the truck. It was only Angel.

"Good to see you, "she said. "I'm glad you ain't make a bitch wait till tonight." She went in her pocket, pulling out a wad of bills. "You brought that for me baby boy? I hustled you up close to two grand."

Calvin's eyebrows rose. He accepted the cash, and tossed her what he'd fixed up prior to leaving the crib.

"I stepped on that little shit fifty-times last night, and it still, was rockin' hardcore niggas to sleep. You ain't see the news?"

Angel climbed out and headed toward the alley where she did her thing. In the distance, Calvin saw someone who made him smile. It was Deloris and Briana sitting on a bench at a bus stop. "I'll be right back." Calvin moved fast for a big man.

Nelson sat there observing the scene. His mind couldn't stop grinding out numbers, as junkies roamed the streets searching for an escape from sickness and pain. He smiled seeing Angel from afar serving his product. "I'm about to fuck this game to death with Dope Dick," he whispered to himself.

Meanwhile, Calvin was hugging Briana. Her big beautiful smile made his morning. But Deloris was still acting stank.

"I'm headed to pick up some things for Momma to make for breakfast before she goes to the funeral," said Deloris. Her face was swollen. Both her eyes black. On her feet, Calvin noticed was his mother's slippers.

"Let me give y'all a ride."

"No thank you," she snapped. "Go be with that white hoe you kissed in front of us."

"I'm comin' to spend some time with you later. Okay?"

She twisted her lips. "Whatever."

Calvin pulled up the wad of money Angel had given him. He put it in Bri's tiny hand. Kissed her and said, "Buy you and your mom something baby. I love you."

"I love you too, Daddy."

***

The rumor mill was buzzing like a chain saw this morning and cutting open both old, and fresh wounds. Today was Camille's funeral and Momma planned to attend it as a show of support, and unity. Violence had been ravaging the neighborhood since as far anyone could remember.

Her phone had been blowing up all morning. Online, someone posted a copy of the police report from the hotel shooting of Pastor Scott. In the report Deloris' name emerged as the pastor's mistress. The pastor's wife was having a nervous breakdown to also discover that Briana's name was listed as one of the beneficiaries on a life insurance policy the pastor had taken out years prior.

Deloris and Briana had returned from the grocery store with five shopping bags, Momma was flipping pancakes as she held her cellphone up to her ear. The gossip was too juicy to resist. Her eyes cut across the living room at Briana who was coming her way with a handful of cash. "Well, Sister Gloria I'll be waiting on you. Sad we're seeing another young life going into a grave." Momma sighed, looked at her time-worn watch, and said "shoot, I'm running late."

"Is everything okay Momma?" asked Deloris, sensing the change in her vibe.

'Well, come fry this sausage chil'. I got to get dressed." She walked towards her bedroom. Briana followed.

Deloris agitated the frying pan by shaking the sizzling meat around. She felt better. Physically at least. Inside her heart ached, and her soul longed from a normal life. She closed her eyelids, only to see Pastor Scott's face just as bullets ripped it apart. The kitchen began to fill with smoke. And the chirping of the smoke detector returned her from the darkness of her horrible daydream.

Momma came out, dressed to impress and took control of the frying pan. "Move chil'." She turned the oven's flame off. "I didn't know how to mention this to you Deloris. Some mess is goin' around online about you and Pastor Scott having had…having an affair. Something about you being at the hotel when…he passed."

"What?"

"Yes. Don't let rumors get you down. You been through way more than enough already. Stress'll kill you."

A horn blared in the distance, and right away Momma headed for the front door. With her bottom lip pushed out, Briana followed behind her. But Momma turned around and said, "stay here and comfort your mother. Tonight we'll bake you a cake."

"Yes ma'am."

***

At the moment, Angel's apartment was a mini lab. Nelson and Calvin had spent four straight hours finessing the precise cutting equation to where the drug dosage wouldn't be fatal. The dope was just that damn powerful. The body count was already at eight and junkies were travelling from all over to buy it.

This investment in time gave Nelson the insight into where he should be at when pressing the pills when he got back to West Virginia. One box back home, when cut, would make 400 boxes. And the Dope Dick would still be just a hair away from deadly.

Angel took mental notes, in fact, she had plans to cut the product ever more. From the way Calvin was talking she would be a major player in this operation. From dealers to hardcore users, she knew everybody. Calvin hit her hand with 14-grams, and he and Nelson exited her bedroom. Angel's daughter was now in the living room. She was scribbling raps in a notebook, with a set of headphones on. Her head moved in sync with whatever she was listening to.

Before they could walk out Angel said, "that there's my daughter."

The girl stood up, shimmied her too-tight boy shorts out the crack of her ass. "who yall?" The young goddess was mixed, with an incredible body. If she wasn't five-nine in height, she was damn close to it.

"I'm Cal, this my nigga right here Nail-head Nelson," joked Calvin. He was looking at the spot of blood on his bandages that had soaked through.

"Oh," the girl said. "I'm Red. On stage I'm Redrum."

Nelson enjoyed the view of Red's rearend and smiled.

"Nice meeting you, shorty. We was on our way out."

Nelson and Sharon had left Chicago, headed back to try to clip some lose ends in West Virginia. Beneath the Dior comforter, all curled up is where Jess was, with a Netflix movie playing. Shopping bags, clothes, and all new high-end necessities was everywhere. Jess had done Calvin much justice by elevating his wardrobe to the moon. "You okay bae?" Calvin sat beside her on the bed.

"No. I am not. I'm dope sick." She wiped a stray tear off her face. "But I'm going to fight it. I promised myself. Nelson, and Sharon I would detox." After a pause, she cooed "Don't you want to go clean too?"

"The idea never crossed my mind. But if you striving to dry out, I'm down for you."

"If I'm sober, I can be a better woman for you. A better friend, lover, maybe wife. Here in Chicago, I saw my competition. These women ain't in barefoot, selling pills for a man like you, I've got to step it up, and keep myself up. I was truly embarrassed to have your mother see me so out of it last night."

Calvin's cellphone started buzzing. He swiped the screen, stood up. "Looks like you're in for the night. Are you?" he asked Jess.

"I'll be just fine. I've got demons to fight. I'm tired of being a slave to dope?"

Calvin leaned down, told her he loved her, gave Jess a long kiss and bounced. He was content with her staying home, he didn't have a use for her being out in the streets no how. It was obvious though. Nelson had chewed her ass out about her decision to move, yet in Calvin's eyes it was the best decision of her life.

The text he'd received was from Angel's phone. After jumping in Jess's Navigator, Calvin called her and drove off. "Angel?"

"This her daughter, Red. You was here earlier. You forgot something. Pull up."

He brought the young goddess' shape and face to mind. "What'd I forget?"

"Me." There was a long pause.

"I'ma see you around, Red. I'm on a mission tonight." He ended the call and parked in front of his mother's apartment, then killed the engine.

Deloris came out just as Calvin was coming up to the walk. She had her hair all done up and her lips covered in a seductive shade of peach. And her fingernails were French tipped. "You're all the way up aren't you? Her eyes zeroed in one on the big rims on the Navigator. "Damn."

"I ain't out here playin'."

"I hear that." She smiled. "Can we go somewhere to talk and be alone?" Deloris headed to the truck.

"Where's Briana at?"

"Momma got her up there teaching her how to bake a pineapple cake."

They got in the truck and merged into the night. "What's up? You seem out of it?"

"A lot's been going on. People saying this, saying that. Have you talked to Momma today?" Her facial expression pleaded for a 'no', which she got, except he simply shook his head. Calvin smelled just like new money, and like a magnet, she was pulled in by it. Seeing they had history it was natural.

"I been busy, why? Momma alright?"

"She's fine. Your female friend's funeral was today. She went." Deloris let out some hot air, there was so much she needed to say. "First, thank you for the money you gave Briana. She gave me half. Then Momma the other half, and realized she had nothing left, and asked me for two dollars." Deloris laughed. "She's my world."

"Mine too."

The way the bass was hitting in the cabin of the SUV loosened Deloris up. And then a very familiar slow jam came on. She turned it up. Baby oh, that's my shit right there! You know I love baby-making music." Deloris sat there, legs parted, rolling her hips slow. "Yes, that's my shit."

This slick bitch know I love when she moves her body that way, thought Calvin. He refused to give her the satisfaction of knowing she was arousing him.

She took both hands, still winding slow and caressed her breast. "I love Jagged Edge. This song gets me wet, and in the mood."

By now, his erection was telling on him like a snitch. He could feel her eyes looking right at it. He had a serious thing for Deloris. They shared many ups and downs. And a child. A beautiful little girl, thought Calvin. And in spite of what he was about to do to her tonight, he still loved her. He hated her too. The line between the two was blurry. Calvin kept his thoughts where they needed to be, giving her the Dope Dick, he knew she desired, and deserved.

"When you raped me, did you enjoy it?"

"You must want me to pull over and put you out?"

She laughed. "I hope that's what I'm getting tonight," she whispered, playing her hand like a true manipulator. "I can't front, I need that."

Calvin glanced over at her and laughed.

"What's funny?" She pulled one of her breasts up, and kissed it through the outside of her blouse. "Do me however you want to, have your way. Beat my ass, dog me. I fucked up and I deserve it." She bit her bottom lip. "Punish me. But when you're done, love me like you always have. I'm the type of bitch that's been spoiled all my life, Calvin. You know that. You can't give me much freedom. A bitch like me got to be on short chain. I never stopped loving you."

Calvin slowly steered into the Red Roof Inn. This long-awaited moment had finally presented itself. Dope sickness was looming over him now, maybe the eagerness of fulfilling his lust for revenge made him feel this way.

"Do you forgive?" she asked, sincerely.

No reply was forthcoming. He parked.

Deloris folded her arms across her chest, wondering what was on Calvin's mind. She knew he was going to snap the fuck out when she let all the skeletons out her closet tonight. But things couldn't get any worse than they now were.

Chapter 18

Giving Briana chocolate cake at night was a regret Momma was beginning to have as the 10 o'clock news continued airing its broadcast about the manhunt still under way for Mike. Briana jumped up and down on the bed beside her. "Girl if you don't sit your butt down or go to sleep!" She popped Briana's thigh. "Quit being hard-headed."

The little girl was unfazed, she now found a doll to play with, then sent it sailing across the bedroom where it crashed onto the hardwood flooring. "Superwoman!" yelled Briana. She laughed, sprang off the bed in happy search of the doll but the: Bam! Bam! Bam! at the front door startled her. Momma too.

Echoing throughout the apartment was the sound of the doorknob rattling, followed by an intense series of knocks. While getting from underneath of the covers, Momma grunted and started fiddling around in her nightstand. She came up with blued-steel, snub-nose .38 Special. "Wait here, chil'." She inserted the pistol down into the pocket of her robe and tossed her wig on. The pounding at the door continued. She crept toward the front door. The person on the other side held a finger over the peep hole. Momma clutched the left side of her chest but that did not settle down the racing of her heart. "Who's there?"

There was silence.

"Me. Michael. Is Deloris here?"

"Who?" She squinted, peering out. The hand that was once there vanished. Mike stood there.

"Open the door!" He rattled the doorknob, "I need to talk with Deloris now! I heard Briana in there."

Momma clutched the handle of the revolver tight. Thumbing back the hammer. The door shook violently on its hinges. "She not here! Leave, get on away from here this time of night."

Just then she heard the clamor of descending footsteps going towards the front door of the apartments, down the stairwell. She peeped out of the window blinds, noticing Mike's shadow and the blackness of night becoming one in the distance.

***

The pulse of this evening was not what Deloris had painted in her imagination. She anticipated an unforgettable asswhippin' and a revenge-fuck and pussy-battering, for her betrayal. But as it seemed, Calvin wanted something totally different. After he returned from the bathroom, his hands undressed her and explored her. His handsome dark brown eyes took in all of her before he delighted himself by pulling one of her hard fingertip-shaped nipples into his mouth. He pulled her closer, gripping her face now thrusting his tongue into her mouth. "How could you do me like that?" He sucked her neck now, and used the other hand to stroke up and down the crack of her big healthy ass.

On fire and pulsating, Deloris lifted his shirt off, squeezing his broad mounds of muscle mass across his chest and shoulders. "Baby, I'm sorry."

"With both hands he pulled her hot cakes apart, and they continued groping at each other until Calvin finally spun her like a ballerina onto the bed.

"Give me my dick," she cooed seductively. "For three years I been waiting on it."

Calvin let his sweats drop to the carpet, and pulled down his silk Gucci boxers, freeing a thick and lengthy, fully erect member that made Deloris quiver with goosebumps. Her mouth watered, and her vaginal walls began to contract on their own. Her wetness ran out the slit of her vulva. "This pussy know daddy's home now." Her hand spread her wings to prove it. She was well-primed, and started working a finger across her clit. The whole time never taking her eyes off of his dick. She knew she'd fucked up, but prayed that this night would start a new chapter. There was so much she needed to tell him, and still yet, so much she needed to conceal.

Calvin grinned while watching her finger-fuck herself. She rolled onto her elbows and knees with her ass up, and face down. Her pussy remained parted open, and her two fingers continued working. He stroked his erection, adding more length and firmness. Calvin knew this was her favorite sexual position. But this night was not about her at all. I was not about what *she waited three-years for*. Because she was sucking dick and getting nailed the entire time, while he sat spiritlessly in a white man's prison cell, it was there, he recalled, when he replaced his pain with opioids. And as if it never happened, she expected him to now, forget and forgive her indiscretions. Never! Her death warrant had long been signed. And now, sealed with a kiss, Calvin just placed at the gate of her anus. "I miss this tight shitter on you."

"Prove it."

He'd been masturbating, contemplating; his erection felt heavy, his muscled penis stood proud, black, thick and long. With the palm of his hand, he smacked the right side of her ass.

"Harder, baby!"

He did it again, harder this time. Deloris cried. Calvin reached down for the sack of Dope Dick, and a condom. Using his teeth, Calvin ripped it open, and rolled the lubricated sheath on his penis, and sprinkled his erection from base to head.

Forth, and back, Deloris rocked her hips, eager to feel the joy of Calvin stretching out her sugar walls. But instead, she felt his lips again. "Nigga quit teasing me!" whispered Deloris, growing frustrated. Just then, she finally felt her tightness being invaded by his own thumb. Then, she moaned out, as his penis penetrated her vagina. "Beat it up. Baby, fuck me hard with that big candy stick."

She didn't need to tell him twice. Yet her orders tonight, he would not follow. Slow he pumped, and deep, driving pure, double-digit inches into her sloppy wet pussy. Within six or seven strokes, her climax surfaced out of thin air, the tingling trickled from her toes up her spine to her neck. "You bout to…make…me cummmm!"

His fist held her by the roots of her weave, skin clapped skin, teeth clenched tight, as he rocked her soul loose.

After flipping Deloris onto her back, he decided to taste his brown beauty, at the same time he wanted to look into her eyes. Her tongue dangled from the corner of her mouth. Calvin sucked her clit and fingered her bald slit into a soaking mess. He now mounted her limp trembling body, pounding and snaking as deep and fast as he could, trying his damnedest to send her soul into the afterlife.

Her facial expression showed him an angelic innocence, one he had never seen before in her. Her warm caramel skin tone morphed into a weird purple-brownish one. In mid-thrust, he forced her ankles upward, and then reclined her knees to where they were met by her ears, and hammered away. In out. In out. The aquatic sounds of her pussy being stroked as she squirted pushed Calvin to the brink of a climax, himself.

"Augh! Augh! Shit! Fuck!" yelled Calvin, releasing his pent-up rage. His dick yanked repeatedly as he came. "Augh! Ugh!" He shuttered, decelerated his humps to a slow grind, allowing his breathing to fall back into a normal rate. After allowing her legs to plop down, he kissed her open mouth. "Deceitful bitch," he said. "I hate myself for loving you."

When Calvin finally walked out of the hotel room, it was pouring down and thunder shook the earth with booming claps. He enjoyed the night but knew he had to get home to his sweet fortune cookie. For now, his job here was done.

Methodically and slowly, Calvin felt was the best way of murdering a woman you hated but loved. Forced by feelings of ambivalence, he turned back to examine his work. Pitiful, naked and sore, she stirred around in bed. "I'll be back later." He closed the door, ambled into the front desk area of the hotel and paid the room up for a week.

***

It had been the worst night of her life. The white horse had tormented Jess to the ends of her existence. She had screamed and cried like an infant until she was nearly voiceless. "My entire body tightened into a knot. Every muscle cramped till I couldn't move!" cried Jess. Calvin held her snug against his chest. "What's that smell?" she asked, animatedly.

"I stopped off at the gym, worked out."

"Gyms stay open all night?"

"Of course," he replied. "I was about to ask you the same damn thing. It smells like shit in here." Calvin opened a window in the bedroom. "Damn!"

"My stomach. I haven't been able to control my bowl movements. I've been spilling my guts out of both ends."

Calvin left out and returned with a cold glass of water. "Drink it."

She did, the entire glass.

Straining to get up, Jess pulled all of the bedding off the bed, and took it all and tossed it on the floor of the laundry room. "This is going to be a challenge of a lifetime," she said. "Nelson made it home safe. And sent his love."

Calvin nodded, then ran himself and Jess a strawberry and vanilla-scented bubble bath. His first bath since being released. He ordered her to take a small bump while in the tub to ease her debilitating dope sickness. Hanging halfway out of his sweat pants pocket was a familiar-looking vial of Naloxone. Jess noticed it just as she began to drift into an all-embracing state of narcosis. "Who is that for?" she asked just before the back of her head hit the edge of the tub.

"I stabbed a disloyal bitch to death with Dope Dick and brought her ass back, so I can kill her again and again, later."

Jess heard him, but she really didn't. She was gone… for the moment.

Chapter 19

With his AK-47 in his clutches, Calvin ascended the stairwell like a character on *Call of Duty*. He placed his ear up to his mother's door. Then knocked.

After their phone conversation earlier about all the secrets and lies, and deception going on behind his back, he and Jess shot straight over to her apartment.

Momma opened the front door, "There's my sonny." She embraced him, as did Briana.

"That's a gun, Daddy," said Briana.

"I know sweetheart, Momma, yall got yall stuff packed? Come on, let's go!" He ushered them out. They were going out to the Lake Forest condo to stay for a while until he found her some new living arrangements far from the ghetto. With a few bags that Jess helped them with, both Momma and Briana climbed up into the Hummer. Jess scooted behind the steering wheel; she knew Calvin was staying behind, but Briana didn't.

"Daddy you're not coming with?"

Calvin craned his head into the window with his lips pursed for a kiss. Briana gave it to him. "I got some business to handle here. I'll be there later. I love you."

He stood there watching the truck pull away. At a distance, he could see a long dope line leading into the alley. After taking the assault rifle inside, he came back out. Junkies were going and coming, being dope sick was a bitch. Calvin knew about the agony first hand. He'd brought Angel more supply, she would just need to step on it first. He headed towards Red in an all-black sweat suit, she was hoodied up, rocking side to side, hands in her pockets. She headed his way with a smile.

"It's been like this all damn night, until now. Ma got me on security, running to the crib every thirty-minutes. I know I done lost weight. This keeps up, I ain't gone have no booty left."

"You funny shorty." Calvin chuckled. "Later today we need to have a serious sit-down and tighten shit up around here."

"Good," said Red. "Them niggas we put out of business ain't feeling the way you fuckin' the game, and putting they ass to shame, cause we know they dope too-touched and lame, Redrum looking for fame."

Calvin smiled. The young woman was all natural, and beautiful, and could rhyme her ass off.

"Put me on," said Red. "Be my manager. I got mad flow, and I'll body a hoe. Bring you the dough, so we ain't gotta slang blow no mo'."

Calvin nodded. She reminded him of a younger Keisha Cole, mixed with Meg the Stallion, but sexier. She pushed a blunt between her full lips and lit it up. "I love your style."

"It's over with!" yelled Angel. "For now it's all gone. Check back later."

"God damn!" growled an angry old black man. "I broke into three houses last night to get some money, then waiting in this long muddafuckin' soup line! You run the fuck out?" The fiend whipped out a long switch blade, twirled it in his hands, then gripped it. He headed right for Angel. But before he could, a single clap of gunfire dispersed the crowd, including Calvin who got low and scurried at a distance.

Red had put a big hole in the back of the man's head. He crashed to the ground.

"When you can, come to the house!" hollered Angel. Mother and daughter sprinted in stride, side by side toward the other end of the alley. Red started jogging backwards. "Dope Dick turn bad bitches into shooters, move the crowd like Eric B, when I bust the Ruger!"

Calvin was in awe. He then began to observe two other junkies rifling through the pockets of the dead man. He fled. Upon reaching the apartment building he saw the woman that he loved, but hated even more. It was Deloris climbing out of a taxi cab. He yelled out her name and she came into his arms.

***

Mike sniffled. His tears came down in torrents, soaking his blood-speckled shirt. He rested his head on the steering wheel of a stolen Buick. Love had dealt him a bad hand. To see Deloris in Calvin's arms after all he'd gone through over this past week shattered his heart all over again. From a distance, he stared at the older apartment building, thanking himself for pulling back up when he did. "Backstabbing bitch!"

He pulled the chicken and biscuit sandwich off the passenger seat and bit into it. But the demonizing thought of Deloris making love to another man caused him to vomit. He didn't bother to wipe the foul-smelling bile off his clothing. Instead, he removed the shirt and tossed it into the backseat. The gashes across his back were still raw, and painful, and more than likely infected by now. This however, did not even come close in comparison to the agony of a broken heart.

The .45 he had held just a single bullet. The thought of putting the slug in his head flashed through his mind as he sat there stuck on stupid. His younger sister Vanessa came to mind, she was serving life down at Tutwiler women's prison in Alabama for murdering her cheating spouse.

Mike curbed his suicidal thoughts. *Who would make sure Sis is taken care of?* He smiled, thinking about his sister. "So who gets this bullet?" he whispered to the gun. "Deloris or her baby's daddy?" For a while he pondered on it, nobody ever made him feel as loved as Deloris had. He could hear her voice echoing in the darkness of his mind, saying "I love you."

Chicago Police cars came into view, five cars deep, and went into the alley. Then a Cook County Coroner's van too, Mike fired up the Buick and took off in a hurry. He stalked his prey from the top of the block now. The odds of delivering vengeance to the very man who had stolen his life were greatly in his favor; odds way too irresistible. This chance, he knew would not present itself ever again. With the hunger for death and the eye of a tiger, Mike focused on the apartment building and nothing else. Now, it was all just a waiting game.

***

Briana and Momma both loved the condominium, it was spacious and spotless. And Momma was already in the island-style kitchen cooking and cleaning. She knew exactly how to detoxify Jess. The thought of it caused her to sigh, the remedy would require a month of gut-wrenching torment, will power and prayer.

Jess walked into the kitchen with Briana at her heels. "Thank you Mom for staying here with us, and offering to help me battle my addiction. I want you to order whatever you need to furnish your and Briana's bedroom. I put fifty-thousand in your closet."

Momma gave Jess a warm appreciative hug and finished cooking. She brought to mind the dark days when Calvin's father waged war on his heroin addiction. She cringed at the thought, then looked up at the ceiling, as if looking into heaven. "Calvin senior your baby boy sure knows how to pick 'em. Show me the way."

Just then, Briana ran up to Momma, yanking at her arm. "Grandma, Jess is in the bathroom throwing up!" She pulled Momma down the long hallway. "She's sick look!" She pointed at Jess; who was on her knees. Head in the toilet.

Chapter 20

When Deloris told Calvin that Briana was not his biological daughter he lost his mind and began sending slaps and a punch that sent Deloris tumbling across the living room floor. More than anything, he was furious with himself for having a heart and reviving her "heartless ass" last night.

He stood over her, "can't keep your fucking legs closed huh, bitch?" He lifted his foot ready to stump her world into the empty apartment below. "I'm about to stamp Gucci on your face!" Before his size 13 could come down, the front door exploded open and Calvin's hands went straight up.

The red-eyed, shirtless man aiming the pistol moved swiftly with animal-like stealth, cracking Calvin across the face with the gun. "Bitch ass nigga, get on your knees."

Clutching the crease on his face, Calvin relented, dropping down onto his knees. But he was kicked in his stomach. This whole time he thought the home-invader was a cop. Deloris' screams made the room spin.

"Bitch, if you scream again, a bullet's going in your face!" said Mike. "Now stand up!"

Calvin took a peek through the blood pouring from his forehead at the intruder who was pulling Deloris into a hug. He kissed her. Then he compassionately studied the way Calvin had swollen and bruised her face.

Deloris cried uncontrollably, while Mike shut the front door and bolted it. Then he commenced to punting Calvin's head like a football. "I couldn't wait! To. Kill. Your. Bitch. Ass!" grunted Mike, stomping Calvin as if he were a cockroach.

"Stop Mike!" screamed Deloris. "Please Mike, no baby. No!"

But Mike was deaf, dumb and blind to everything but inflicting life-draining punishment to the fresh-out-of-prison home-wrecker, squirming on the floor. "Go! To! Sleep!" Mike continued showering Calvin with kicks.

"Ugh!" moaned Calvin, finally catching hold of Mike's foot as it came down toward his near-fractured skull again. He twisted it, sending Mike splattering onto the glass coffee table. The gun flew out his hand. Calvin, in spite of his semi-conscious state crawled on top of Mike, delivering a series of face-crushing punches, most missed. The last two connected like an ax chopping wood. Blood spattered across the living room walls.

Mike ate the flurry of punches like popcorn, each one less impactful than the one before. Calvin was winded. Mike pulled down one of his wild punches and gator-rolled Calvin onto his back and clamped both his hands around Calvin's throat. "You's a pussy!"

Chest strength was Calvin's strongest point. He pushed Mike up into the air with ease, until Mike kneed him in the balls twice for good measure. "She's my bitch!" yelled Mike as loud as he could, calling upon his every ounce of inner strength. He wanted to hear the 'pop!' His neck rippled like tree roots, his arms trembling. "Auuuhh!"

The thrust from Calvin's hips sent Mike and his strangulation grip flying into the wall head first. Neither man could hear Deloris screaming. She held the AK-47 in her hand, unable to figure out how to disengage the safety. She tossed it aside. "Stop! Stop!"

Mike's pistol found its way back into his grip. But Calvin was hell bent on taking it away. Both men, bathed in blood, found themselves in a vicious life or death struggle as they grappled and strained to keep the barrel of the gun from aiming at them.

"My bitch! My!" said Mike. "Bitch!" The powerful head butt Mike delivered was perfectly-timed. It put Calvin flat on his back.

The room spun, Calvin's chest heaved up and down. Blood poured out his nose. His vision blurred. Trained at his head now was a big pistol. The man behind the trigger held Deloris at his side. "This here bitch belong to me motherfucker!" Blood poured from his mouth.

Calvin had no options now but to simply embrace death. "Fuck you and that stankin' hoe!" Deloris tried to squiggle free to no avail, Calvin stared at her, she would be the last thing he saw. He dared not to move, savoring every second of life he had remaining. He knew this was the end.

Mike inched closer for a dead-center headshot, as Deloris broke loose, screaming and crying. "Did you hear me pussy nigga? That there stankin' no good bitch is mine!"

"She community pussy nigga. I beat the pussy and ass up last night."

Mike stomped Calvin in the nuts, then he did it again. Calvin squalled in pain. "That's my pussy!" He stomped him again, "Say it!" said Mike. "Say it!"

Calvin refused to say anything.

Mike trained the firearm at his forehead, his finger cupped the curve of the trigger. He heard footsteps coming his way fast. Only to feel the piercing sting of a twelve-inch butcher knife slam deep into the left side of his chest! Just the handle was visible, but it too became blood-soaked; a fountain of blood gushed out. The fatal blow dislodged his pistol almost. Mike crumbled to his knees raised the gun up at Deloris' chest. "Why baby? I thought you loved me?" The pistol shuddered in his grip.

Boc!

His body hit the floor with a loud thump, right beside Calvin, who remained in a ball, holding his dick. He was barely able to stand and ultimately, he gained control of himself with the help of Deloris.

The two of them staggered together to Angel's apartment. It felt like it took forever to get there.

Angel opened the front door, and Calvin collapsed to the floor of her living room.

"I'm forever yours, baby should I call a paramedic?" said Deloris.

"Hell no. Call Momma."

Chapter 21

The next month had its ups and downs like the stock market but all in all, things were going smooth. Momma had gotten Jess clean, marvelously, yet turned her out on soul food. Jess had put on about 20 pounds in all the places that draws a black man's attention.

Deloris was claiming to be four-weeks pregnant, and had become friends with Red. They both disposed of Mike's body, tossing it into an abandoned house on 63rd Street. Red had inspired Deloris to sing, and she discovered the voice she never knew was there.

The Dope Dick founder was sexually inactive; his testicles were swollen to the size of apples, and his penis developed an abnormal curve to it. Calvin purchased a distressed building not far from his condo for a shade over 200K, cash. It was to be Redrum Music Group LLC. There was 300-grand in recording equipment just waiting to be installed soon.

It didn't take long for Nelson to get into another situation with the wolves out of Detroit. He'd gotten shot again. This time in the thigh and ass during a botched robbery attempt. He offered 100K to anyone who'd put either of those involved in a casket. Calvin had no interest in the hit, it wasn't worth his time, not with Jess thinking clearly now, and with all the cash pouring in.

Against his wishes, Jess got back in game, and teamed back up with her brother who was now shipping her the Dope Dick pills. Jess had the uppity white folks on lockdown, and was bringing in fifty times more than Angel was. Jess was clocking two-hundred grand a day, and you couldn't tell her she wasn't the shit, it would only be a few more days before her new Mercedes truck would arrive from Germany.

Calvin bought Momma a similar, if not nicer condo across the street from a Chicago Bears defensive tackle who got traded to Miami. Momma required her space, especially when Calvin started having both Jess and Deloris in bed at the same time, every now and then.

Jess had always fantasized of being intimate with a black woman, and a reality is what Calvin made it. He had yet to join them, but was looking forward to it when he healed up. It killed him, watching two wet, brown and cream-colored pussies slow-grinding together, and not be able to fuck them both. Life was good. Except for one thing.

Calvin's supervised release officer couldn't be bought off. With all the Dope Dick in the world, it was impossible to fuck the federal system. He hired a lawyer, who advised him to turn himself in. "Ain't no way." He slammed the phone down. It was hard to get comfortable with a prison sentence looming in the shadows. "Fuck the feds!" he shouted.

Briana stayed at Momma's most of the time, as did Deloris, except for when she wanted to hook up with Jess.

Jess had her strung out on Dope Dick now, and practically eating out of her hand.

***

Calvin smiled. He stood beside Red in the studio checking out the progress of things. They walked into what would be the recording booth. "About two more weeks we'll be recording in this bitch." Calvin sat on a box after dusting it off somewhat.

Red bounced, and rocked her shoulders. "I can't wait, God, I swear this is a dream come true. Thank you for believing in me. I really mean it." Red lit a blunt of Train Wreck she pulled out her purse.

"You talented. I know you're going to blow up." He received the blunt, hit it hard. Calvin coughed. Handed it back.

"Thank you." She stood in front of him, and started a seductive swaying of her hips. "Am I sexy to you?"

"Ain't no question." He smiled, slanted-eyed. "You bad, shorty. You got that look the industry loves."

"Why you never tried to get in my panties before then? I mean, I know you got a hot woman at home, and Deloris too. Me and Deloris talk you know." She batted her bedroom eyes. Then she cradled his head in between her two soft breasts. "I'm your product, and I think you ought to sample me." She kissed his nose. "Sample me, please."

Red took a couple steps backwards, did her dance. Next her skirt lifted up revealing a flawless round yellow ass. His hands began to reach out. Caressing her, pulling her on his lap. She blew him a shotgun, then tamped the blunt out on the unfinished concrete floor.

"It's crazy," said Calvin. "Your pretty face, tender young body. I can tell you ain't been through the ringer of no-good motherfuckers. Tell me about you, Red?"

The sounds of hammering, drills, ladders being clanked against things filled the air, which allowed Red the opportunity of whispering in his ear. Before she did, his four-karat solitaire earring held her speechless for a second. "You okay?" he asked.

"Well, at twelve I started writing music to escape my Mom and Dad. My dad's white by the way, they would always fight. My dad was my Mom's favorite John. I guess she was smoking crack heavy. She'd been gone for days. One night she came home in the middle of the night and dad beat her senseless. I knew where his gun was. So I shot and killed him. I was sent to a juvenile detention facility until I turned 18.

I ain't been out too long. I'm a full-blooded virgin. Only things that's ever been up in me is tampons and every now and then I finger myself." She giggled, holding up her middle finger, moving it in circles.

In the most sensual way, Red put her lips up to his, and straddled him. They kissed for a while, while Red slowly worked her center grindingly against Calvin's failing erection. Penetration was something she never had, but Red knew how to get off. "I'm still—"

"I know you still healing, but you can still eat my pussy." She eased Calvin onto the floor. Removed her panties, and squatted down on his chest so he could see it. And smell it. "Fresh and shaved. Never fucked. Never ate. Make it yours."

"Shorty."

"Shhh! Don't say nothing."

Red scooted closer toward his face and started riding it, she didn't stop till she climaxed.

***

Angel's small apartment was circled by police donned in all black paramilitary gear. They pounded on her door hard. "Chicago Police! We got a warrant!" Boom! Boom! Boom!

Angel filled her small glass stem with a piece of crack. With a lighter, she struck a flame, and hit it. Then she exhaled. The plate full of small yellow rocks in front of her, she dumped into a sandwich bag. Next, she tied it into a tight knot and stuffed it into her vagina. By the time she exited here bedroom, the cops were storming inside. And an infrared laser landed dead on her chest. "Bitch, don't you fuckin' move!"

Another cop yelled. "Get your hands in the air! Get down! Now!"

Angel obeyed the orders of the lawmen. She knew, aside from the crack she'd hidden in her hot box, there was not any other drugs in the crib. There was a backpack she was certain they would find. It contained sixty-five thousand. On the floor is where she rested her weary head. The sounds of them tearing her shit apart; it was like fingernails scratching a chalkboard. More than anything, she hated cops.

A thin, older grey-haired white woman walked up, she squatted to Angel's level. She wasn't uninformed, but had a gold badge fashioned to her belt. She looked to be an alcoholic.

"My name is Mrs. Hardimon. Do you know why I'm here, Angel?" asked the woman. In her hand was a mugshot photo of Angel.

"Mmm." Angel closed her eyes, and probed her mind for an answer. She had lived a criminal lifestyle since the age of ten.

"I'm a homicide detective." She motioned for two male officers to stand her up. One of the men clicked on a set of handcuffs, securing Angel's hands behind her back. They tugged her onto the sofa where the pillow had been flipped out, "Sit down."

The detective moved closer. "I was assigned to work a cold case three weeks ago. A homicide. One from sixteen-years back, okay?"

Angel shook her head up and down.

"Two white males working undercover were looking to buy a kilogram of cocaine. They were both bound and murdered execution-style. The buy money was stolen. Before the men were slain, one of them fought with the attacker. Beneath his fingernails, the deceased left us a clue. A blueprint. In fact, I'd say he left us an undisputed declaration, pointing, as if on the witness stand to who killed him. Do you understand how DNA works?"

"Yeah." Tears welled up in Angel's eyes and spilled out. The release was overwhelming.

"The dead may get buried, but the spirit of the dead never die. Never, Angel. Now, I am going to ask you, right here, and now. Did you do it?"

For a long while, Angel said nothing. Her bottom lip trembled. "I was there." Angel sighed, lowered her head. "But I didn't pull the trigger and kill them."

"From my recent investigation of you, the streets say they call you 'Angel' because you used to turn men into ghosts. Is that true?"

Angel closed her eyes, shook her head slowly up and down, feeling the tremendous weight of guilt lift from her tormented soul. Another officer came into view holding a pistol, sealed in a clear evidence envelope. "This is all we found, along with a bag of cash."

The homicide detective examined the pistol. "Is this yours?" She looked over at Angel.

"Yeah."

She handed the gun back to the cop who had found it in Red's bedroom. "A single round is missing."

"I think you ought to turn it over to Operation Legend, this neighborhood has had eleven gun-related murders in the past week."

"Good idea." He gripped the radio connected to his bulletproof vest, rambled some code-words and walked off.

During the ride down to the Cook County Jail, Angel took in her final view of Chicago. She knew her chances of ever seeing daylight again was slim to none. For one, the triggerman in that murder was dead and gone. Red has shot and killed him, her abusive husband. So maybe there was some hope, if only a little.

***

Calvin's nose provided the perfect piece of warm flesh for Red to grind her clit against. And in doing so, fast and steadily she experienced the magic of multiple orgasms. Six in fact, each one left her thighs quivering, and her vagina ejaculating like a water gun.

And all Red wanted now was for Calvin to bust her cherry. She groped a hand behind her slow-rolling hips, feeling the girth and length of his semi-erection. "I need to feel this...this big submarine up in my ocean."

"Have patience baby girl." He sat up, and pulled her into a kiss, then placed each breast back into her bra.

Calvin's cellphone had been blowing up, and he was done sampling Red. As far as he was concerned, she was a smash hit in every way. He wiped his face off with his hand and forearm. "You tried to drown me shorty."

She giggled. "I hope you don't think I was peeing on you. I'm embarrassed." She fixed her attire, looked at herself in her small clutch mirror and closed it up. She was shocked by the way her thighs still trembled, and too, how in love she now was.

Calvin swiped through all his missed calls, and texts. He placed the phone up to his ears, panic-stricken.

Jess answer—ed, crying and screaming.

Chapter 22

Jess had only had her showroom-new Mercedes G-Wagon for an hour when she got the disturbing call from Sharon saying that Nelson had been arrested. His bond was set at five-hundred-grand cash, and Jess knew exactly where to get it from in one of Nelson's West Virginia stash houses.

As her flight attendant smiled at her, then kindly asked passengers to "buckle up," Jess figured the plane would be landing in Huntington soon, she was right; the bird sliced through a pocket of turbulence and graciously touched down at Tri State Airport. There, she rented a Chevy truck.

Jess had the cash at home, easily. But she well-knew she couldn't fly with it. She couldn't believe how things had gone from sugar to shit. And just being back here made her nose drain, and stomach cramp, as her body began to yearn for the days, she thought she'd left behind.

The drive through the darkness to this half-empty, secluded home took up every bit of an hour. Inside, Jess moved swiftly to the wall vault, tossing fifty ten-thousand-dollar rubber-banded knots into a trash bag she found in the kitchen. Before leaving out, she closed the vault back up, set the alarm system, and headed to Huntington. Jess didn't give a shit about Calvin's warning about coming here, Calvin was the one still using, not her, she thought. This was her brother, and rotting in jail was something he was not about to do if she could help it, period!

The streets looked similar to the Walking Dead, pale-white bodies beat their bare feet in search of the pale white horse. Jess tried to ignore the trail of thin white prostitutes straggling in the blackness near the Huntington library. Any one of those young girls could so easily have been her. If she could, she would take each and every one of them up to Momma to be fixed, and healed before their fate became fatal.

When her cellphone rang it startled her. It was Calvin. "Hey love, I'm here. I miss you already."

"I do too, bae, you be careful. I get a bad vibe about the trip, Jess straight up."

"You're paranoid," said Jess. "I'm going to call you back just as soon as I post his bond. I'm pulling up now love." Jess ended the call, tossed the phone on the seat beside her. Then steered into an empty parking space. She pulled the bag of cash into her lap, but before Jess could step foot out of the vehicle, the feds were all over her ass like a tight skirt on a two-dollar hooker.

They yanked her out. Removed the cash bag.

"We've been waiting for you, Jessie. You're under arrest," said an agent of the DEA. "We finally got you."

"For what?"

"You'll find out when your federal indictment is unsealed by Judge Goldman in court tomorrow. That is, unless you might want to cooperate with us." The agent led Jess over away from the crowd of officers. "Jessie, listen to me, I know you are a drug addict, dealing with this agonizing demon, and the horrible effects of the drug. Tell me Jessie, please tell me who raped and overdosed that poor pregnant girl and dumped her body? I've got to nail his ass to the cross. Talk to me Jessie."

"Where's my brother?" Jess now trembled. "Where's Nelson?"

"He's in a Regional Jail cell. Right along with his wife, and a slew of his underlings." The agent paused, trying to make eye contact with Jess. He lifted her chin up. "Where is Calvin Jones?"

Chapter 23

Angel had called Red's cellphone collect from the jail after being booked and assigned to a range. But details could not be explained. Angel said, "Go as far as you can away from the nest and you'll be good. Make me proud. I love you."

Red understood, yet she did not, exactly. Meanwhile Calvin pulled into the driveway of the condo, threw the truck in 'park' and jumped out, "Come on!" He moved swift.

Red followed Calvin inside. He vanished down a hallway and came out struggling with three Louis Vuitton duffel bags. He tossed one to Red and they got ghost. When they made it to Angel's apartment, Red skipped into the dark-windowed tenement and emerged with a book bag and notebooks. They pulled off after she got back in.

"Police musta found my gun. Fuck!" said Red. "Shit." She folded her arms across her chest.

"Don't trip," said Calvin. "We taking a little vacation down to Atlanta for a while. This way things can play out while we move forward."

"What about my Mom? She's all I got."

"She get a bond, we'll post it. If not, we'll get her a lawyer. Till then, we'll hit her books with a few bands, shorty."

The ghetto tonight, was alive, junkies searched listlessly for Dope Dick. Yet, it would not be found, at least not in Chicago anyway.

Calvin jumped onto the interstate and eventually merged onto I-65 South. He had been battling his demons and desires. His intestines twisted, and growled. "You okay over there?" asked Calvin. "You all quiet."

"A lot's going on in my head. At the same time, I'm coming up with some lyrics. All I wanted was to make some bread, hit a junkie in his motherfuckin' head with the stick, now I'm riding shotgun with Dope Dick." She looked over at the grin on Calvin's face. "The studio almost done. I was hoping to link up with Durk on a track. Mom's in jail. No bail and I'm trusting you, a total stranger to love me, and protect me."

"Red, be cool. You know what?"

"What?"

"We about to go down to Atlanta and fuck the game every which way we can. You my product, right?"

"Yes."

"Alright then. Forever mine. I protect what's mine. I kill for mine. I grind for mine."

Red smiled, leaned in and kissed him. Then she pulled up a tablet and pen and put her thoughts on paper. While she was in her zone, his phone buzzed. It was his mother's number flashing in the display.

"Glad you called."

"Police is raidin' your place. A bunch of 'em too. Stay where you at. Stay put! I hope they don't come here."

"I hope they don't either." Calvin clutched his stomach. "I'm safe. I love you. I'm out of town. Give Briana a kiss for me."

"I will. I love you too, son."

"Ma, where Deloris at, you heard from her?"

"Sister Mary said she seen her early this morning up and down the street on Seventy-Third, jumping in and out of cars with men. Must be selling her body. Po' chil'. Sad."

The line went silent. Calvin was convinced that Deloris had finally gotten the hand she had called for. Sucking and fucking indiscriminately was her joy, and now she was a slave to whoredom in the ugliest way imaginable.

"You need anything Momma?"

"God takes care of my needs. You stay out of jail, son. And stay alive."

"I will," said Calvin. "If you get a call from Jess, tell her you ain't heard from me."

Chapter 24

Jess used her hand to rake through her hair as if it would calm the stress that caused her head to ache, and stomach to bubble. She stared out behind designer shades, into the cotton-shaped morning clouds. Her plane began to descend towards the runway above Midway Airport, in Chicago.

The landing was a smooth one, but Jess knew the difficulties of what she was up against. It would not be easy or smooth. And the only thing that could cure her soul-crushing dope sickness now was a fix.

With Nelson not willing to turn rat, Jess along with Nelson's wife, Sharon were doing exactly what their benefactors required of them. "We're here." Jess nudged Sharon's arm. Then she dug around inside her purse for her key card. It was there. Jess sighed.

"That was fast." Sharon wiped her mouth, and unbuckled her seatbelt. "Let's go find this son-of-a-bitch, Jessie."

Jessie followed behind Sharon down through the Tarmac and eventually out into the airport parking lot in search of her G-Wagon. "There my baby is." She pointed.

When they parked in front of the condo, the first thing Jess noticed was her Navigator was gone. *And no telling whatever else.* Hanging crooked was the front door. "I feel sick, I bet the place is a mess."

Sharon headed into the condo, and realized just how thoroughly the feds had been in searching the place. She looked to Jess, only to find her vomiting. "Jesus Christ!"

"I'm okay." Jess used her arm to erase the slim off her chin. "I'm okay." She walked inside. "My God. They tore the place apart."

"I'd say," replied Sharon. "Where his mother live?"

"Across the street." Jess headed to the bedroom, discovering their drug stash spot empty. "God, I'm sick!" She pulled the headboard back, then pried open the false backing. "They didn't find the guns."

Sharon reached for the Beretta in Jess's hand, leaving her with the Glock. "I like dis one." She grinned, rubbing a hand across the steel contours of the pistol. "It open up big gash."

"That's fine." Jess held her stomach, "I need something…to… get this ape off my damn back."

"Go ahead." Sharon eased closer to Jess. "Say it. You need some Dope Dick."

"Yeah, I really do." She raked her hair back and gave Sharon a pitiful expression. "I'm sick."

"Where do you think Calvin's at?"

"I don't know. Maybe in the inner city." Jess pulled up her cellphone. She well-knew it was tapped, as did Sharon.

Sharon pointed, signify for her to set the phone down. She did.

"Come." Sharon headed toward the front door, and out into the crisp air. "Show me where his mother lives?" Sharon concealed her pistol in the small of her back, while Jess jacked a round into the chamber, and did the same by concealing it.

Together they headed toward Momma's front door.

"I feel terrible, I got the shivers."

"Quit bitchin'!" Sharon yanked her by the arm. "You're pissing me off, Jess."

Knock! Knock! Knock!

"Okay." Jess frowned. "I've got to shit."

***

Calvin was too tired to drive straight through to Atlanta. And instead, he and Red found a comfortable hotel room off of I-65 in Indianapolis. Red was still asleep, while Calvin had found the services of a young white, freckled-faced prostitute earlier that morning.

In spite of his manhood injuries, he managed to form a semi-erection, and laced his condom-covered penis with the near-pure dope. Calvin had penetrated the whore's tight channel as best he could until her colorless skin turned blue, and she quit breathing. While doing so, and watching her soul escape her body, he visualized her face as Jess's.

Calvin filled the tub with water and carried the soulless street angel from the bed to the bathtub, and lowered her inside the water, pushing her head below.

He flushed the semen-filled condom down the toilet and left the scene of the homicide. Just then, before he could make it back to his room, his cellphone rang. It was his mother's number. "Hey Momma, how are you?"

"I'm giving you thirty-minutes to be here! Not a minute longer bitch. Get here!" yelled a woman with a thick Jamaican accent. "Think I fucking playing, try me!"

Crack!

"Who is this? Who the fuck!"

In the background, Calvin could hear the screaming, the crying, the pain, then the line went dead.

TO BE CONTINUED...

Ecstasy

When Danny's coke-dealing girlfriend, Alexis, is sold a quarter-bird of bad dope, he calls upon the cruel hand of murder to settle the score. Yet, in the fury of the moment, having never considered the eyewitnesses he left alive at the scene, Danny is forced on the run, leaving St. Louis and his girlfriend behind.

While laying low at his uncle's farm in southern Illinois, Danny meets Monica of Shut 'Em Down Kennels and stumbles across Becky, again; a gorgeous blond who lures him deep into the lucrative underworld of ecstasy pills.

With a grand champion bloodline in the works and Becky finally in his bed, Ecstasy Kennels is established, feared, and respected. As the cash pours in like he's never tasted it before, only more and more money can quench his thirst.

Just before a seven-figure dog fight in Detroit, secret indictments come down. Doors are kicked in by the Feds. Loyalties are tested. Danny quickly realizes that either federal prison or death is just a breath away. He must choose his poison, fast! Or call upon murder once again in order to save himself. But killing a loved one isn't as easy as killing an enemy. But it must be done…

No other book in history dares to take you into the dark underground world of pill poppin' and dog fighting.

Ecstasy II

Haunted By The Past

For survival's sake, Danny realizes he must abandon his booming Ecstasy pill operation in exchange for a more honest occupation. Yet the demons of the past prove that they never sleep, they haunt, they prey, and if allowed to, they destroy.

In Becky's eyes, Danny is Godsent, and with his unborn seed forming in her womb, there is nothing in the world she wouldn't do to keep him from the jaws of the prison system.

When old acquaintances appear, envy surfaces, and evil intent rears its ugly head, there is nothing left for a queen to do but checkmate the threat at all cost. But is murder too high of a cost to pay for love?

Ecstasy III

Blood Sisters

Deep within the belly of the criminal underworld there is no worse sin than betrayal. So when Danny's loyalty takes him on an unexpected business trip to Southern California, the wages of his adversary's sins are paid for with swift death and destruction.

As the body count continues to climb in the streets, the Mexican Mob only adds to it after millions of dollars and cocaine come up missing in Atlanta, all of which belongs to them. Yet, they find that tracking down those responsible seems to be an impossible task, because there's more than one group of predators on the prowl.

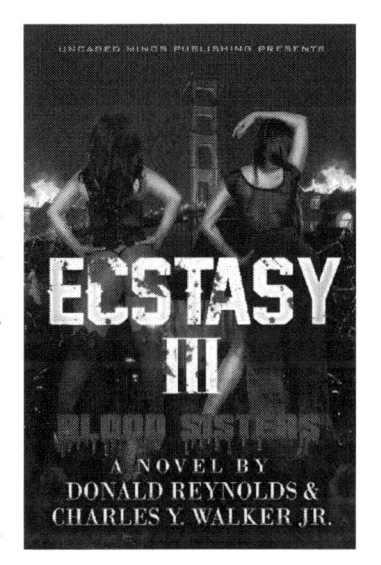

With bullets flying in the South, and blood spilling in the West, will the only ones left standing in the end be blood sisters? Or are the innocent forced to pay for the sins of guilty? Find out in this epic, fast-paced trilogy!

The Ops

After losing his father to a lengthy federal prison sentence, 14-year old Mannie Johnson and his older brother Que realize they're now the heirs of a lucrative drug empire.

Before claiming the throne, Mannie's first test comes as an unexpected stretch in juvenile detention, where he makes a few allies, and one bloodthirsty enemy along the way.

While doing his time, Que's waist-deep in the grimy streets of St. Louis, regulating, expanding, networking, holding things down, establishing rules, setting examples, and learning the hard way that: Everything that looks good, ain't good for you. As he's recovering from a near-fatal ambush, Mannie's released, and he's hungry to do it way bigger than his father ever dreamed of. Mannie's young, restless, fearless, with a set of street laws of his own that he lives by: If you're not with us, you're against us. Being against us, makes you: The OP's... Opposition Beware!

Operation Black Bones

To be a gangster like his uncle West is all Chili wants to be. At his age, fast money and promiscuous girls seems to be the definition of life. But having been sheltered by his grandmother, he knows nothing about the pain, suffering, and bloodshed that comes with the title. Living in the illusion of rap music and urban thralldom, he desires nothing more than to have his opportunity of becoming a real street legend....

But that honor, Chili learns, comes with a price no sum of money can afford. In his quest, Chili not only creates clear and present dangers for all those innocent around him, but he also stirs up those ghosts thought to be dead and gone...

His new dreams give life to old nightmares and leaves a trail of blood so long that those resting peacefully in their graves cry out for justice...

For the past never forgets.

Ghetto Lust

Erotic Obsessions, Twisted Fantasies, Dark Desires, Bi-Sexual Love Affairs, Hot Steamy sex! Brace yourself as you get ready to experience: GHETTO LUST

Ghetto Lust II

A Salacious Collection of Short Urban Erotic Stories

It's no secret, dwellers of the urban ghetto are of a dark subculture where love is a rarity. Within this underworld, love is conditional, and dominated by vice, betrayal and lust. Lust and even more lust...

This raw, hot-blooded compilation of urban erotica lulls you on an unforgettable joyride through the sinful pleasures, and sexual complexities often found, like treasures in the jungles of the ghetto. The place so many call hell, or home. While others call it Heaven. You decide...

Embrace Ghetto Lust, prepare yourself to be consumed by it...again!

Greed Lust & Vengeance

In the grimy slums of Charlotte, North Carolina, two reputed rival drug lords find themselves obsessed with a beautiful, seductive and very pregnant exotic dancer named China, who's also a mistress of deception. Both men, armed and dangerous with extensive histories of violent criminal behavior, discover themselves virtual slaves to their uninhibited lust for the sheer pleasures China gives them. Slugs begin to fly when Raven seeks to unleash his jealous rage upon his sworn adversary, the passionate and charming fugitive Lamont King, for unsuspectingly moving in on his extremely profitable drug turf with a much higher quality of dope. Driven by greed and unable to obstruct Lamont's meteoric rise to power in the drug trade, Raven brings in the help of his gangbangin' cousin and his crew from Memphis's notorious LeMoyne Garden housing projects to settle the score. Meanwhile, Lamont develops a close-knit bond with China's crack-addicted father Irvin, and during the blood-letting and struggle for power, money and China's heart, unexpected circumstances arise that land both Lamont and Irvin in one of the most dangerous and barbaric-like federal penitentiaries in the entire U.S. for an armed bank robbery that they didn't even commit. The direct appeals are timely filed, but will they make it out of prison? And if so, dead or alive? If alive, vengeance is definitely in order

Greed Lust & Vengeance II

Plans are made to murder a federal judge and prosecutor after China's man, Lamont King, and her father, Irvin Rice, are shipped off to a deathly violent U.S. penitentiary to begin serving a lengthy sentence for armed bank robbery. Meanwhile, it's back to the brass-pole and hustling on stage for China. Her career as a stripper in Atlanta is cut short when China's greedy and lustful boyfriend, Diego---a Colombian drug cartel member and enormously successful importer of cocaine---decides he has much bigger and more profitable plans for her. When China suddenly flees in a desperate attempt to reconcile her past, the present and then her future, bodies from inside the prison and those spilling onto the streets are dispatched with swift a vengeance to the morgue. And who, if in fact anyone, can elude the deadly bullets or the acute blade of retribution when karma calls? Only time will tell…

Dope Dick

After a set of loose lips sends Calvin Jones to prison, he begins to see his life more clearly, because those he once vowed his love and loyalty to reveal their true selves.

While walking through the gates of freedom, Calvin does not leave everything behind. Instead, he brings home with him, three-years worth of harbored anger, and a nasty habit he picked up along the way.

For all those who turned their backs on Calvin during his darkest hour, he can't wait to fuck them over! Especially the women, they turned his very heart black.

Although well-endowed, Calvin knows it will take more, for no one alive is strong enough to resist his dope dick.

Sex Slave

Completely unique worlds explode and come crumbling down hard when Mia Jones and Ski Red meet for the first time under dangerous circumstances.

Discovering the security and beauty in one another, neither Ski Red nor Mia desire a return to a life once-lived. And instead, they forge ahead down I-20 West on a bond cemented of sex, murder and life on the lam.

Just before a bank robbery, matters complicate when Ski Red's delusions of converting Mia into his stay-at-home whore reaches a boiling point. Partly because she's everything he has never had before. And she proves to be all he needs to survive. Yet both their survival depends on staying together, and two steps ahead of the feds, and more importantly, a blessing from the cartel, who has the sex trafficking game on lockdown!

The Evil Within

On the outside, Bobbie Watermaker is an All-American man he has a beautiful wife and two lovely kids who adore him. But on the inside, he is a sexual deviant with a strong lust for blood. His wonderful life slowly begins to crumble apart when he fails at murdering a homicide detective investigating the case of one of his victims.

Will Bobbie be able to continue to indulge in his wicked and sick fetish for killing, or will his unbated reign of terror in the city of Columbia, South Carolina be brought to an end?

Join Lavaytron Mills as he takes you on a rollercoaster ride of suspense in this shocking thriller that is The Evil Within.

Book Order

Greed Lust and Vengeance I	$14.99
Greed Lust and Vengeance II	$14.99
Ghetto Lust I	$14.99
Ghetto Lust II	$14.99
The Ops	$14.99
Operation Black Bones	$14.99
Ecstasy	$14.99
Ecstasy II	$14.99
Ecstasy III	$14.99
Juicy's Revenge	$14.99
Dope Dick	$14.99
Sex Slave	$14.99
Evil Within	$14.99

Shipping

Standard Ground (5-7 days) - $2.09

Order Total:

_____

Mail Order to:
Uncaged Minds Publishing
P.O. Box 436
Green Bay, Wisconsin 54305
Uncagedmindspublishing.com

Please be sure to include shipping address

Name: _____

Address: _____

Made in United States
Orlando, FL
06 May 2024